"You Do Know That You'll Have To Stay Here Overnight, Don't You? Maybe Even Longer."

Anxiety flitted around inside Samantha's stomach. It looked as if it would be just the two of them in the house.

"You seem to be uncomfortable," Jace added. "Let me assure you that you're perfectly safe—"

"Oh, no...it's not that."

Samantha stared at the flames in the fireplace. Exactly what was her problem? She had been totally unprepared for any of the things that had occurred since she left Los Angeles. And the biggest surprise of all was the way Jace Tremayne made her pulse race. It was inappropriate, very confusing...and very real. It was also totally absurd. He was a cowboy, a rugged outdoorsman—not at all the type of man who would fit in her world.

And a cattle ranch in Wyoming was certainly no place for her....

Dear Reader,

The celebration of Silhouette Desire's 15th anniversary continues this month! First, there's a wonderful treat in store for you as Ann Major continues her fantastic CHILDREN OF DESTINY series with November's MAN OF THE MONTH, *Nobody's Child*. Not only is this the latest volume in this popular miniseries, but Ann will have a Silhouette Single Title, also part of CHILDREN OF DESTINY, in February 1998, called *Secret Child*. Don't miss either one of these unforgettable love stories.

BJ James's popular BLACK WATCH series also continues with *Journey's End*, the latest installment in the stories of the men—and the women—of the secret agency.

This wonderful lineup is completed with delicious love stories by Lass Small, Susan Crosby, Eileen Wilks and Shawna Delacorte. And *next* month, look for six more Silhouette Desire books, including a MAN OF THE MONTH by Dixie Browning!

Desire…it's the name you can trust for dramatic, sensuous, engrossing stories written by your bestselling favorites and terrific newcomers. We guarantee handsome heroes, likable heroines…and happily-ever-after endings. So read, and enjoy!

Melissa Senate

Senior Editor

Please address questions and book requests to:
Silhouette Reader Service
U.S.: 3010 Walden Ave., P.O. Box 1325, Buffalo, NY 14269
Canadian: P.O. Box 609, Fort Erie, Ont. L2A 5X3

SHAWNA DELACORTE
WYOMING WIFE?

SILHOUETTE *Desire*®
Published by Silhouette Books
America's Publisher of Contemporary Romance

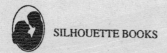

SILHOUETTE BOOKS

ISBN 0-373-76110-4

WYOMING WIFE?

Copyright © 1997 by Sharon K. Dennison

This edition published by arrangement with Harlequin Books S.A.

® and TM are trademarks of Harlequin Books S.A., used under license. Trademarks indicated with ® are registered in the United States Patent and Trademark Office, the Canadian Trade Marks Office and in other countries.

Printed in U.S.A.

SHAWNA DELACORTE

has delayed her move to Washington State, staying in the Midwest in order to spend some additional time with family. She still travels as often as time permits and is looking forward to visiting several new places during the upcoming year while continuing to devote herself to writing full-time.

One

Nowhere in Samantha Burkett's neatly organized and planned-out life had she ever imagined she would someday be in a situation like this one—at the mercy of a complete stranger, strapped into a helicopter seat, and skimming above a frozen landscape toward some unknown destination.

She had never been so cold in all her twenty-nine years. The only impulsive action she had ever taken in her entire life, and look where it had gotten her. She shivered inside her lightweight jacket. One thing was blatantly obvious—the wilds of Wyoming was no place for a tailored silk pantsuit and Italian leather shoes. She was a long way from Los Angeles and the conference-room protocol of the business world where she efficiently functioned on a daily basis.

An entirely new type of fear churned in the pit of her stomach as she watched the ground rush by beneath them. Even though she was strapped in, her side of the two-seater helicopter had no door. Not only was the cold wind whipping right through her thin clothes, she just knew she was going to fall out. She closed her eyes and made an attempt at swallowing the lump in her throat.

A single tear ran down her cheek. She quickly wiped it away. She thought she had cried out every tear that could be squeezed from her body two days ago, when her entire world had come crashing down around her. She shook her head to clear away the bad thoughts. That part of her life was over forever. She had to make a plan for the future. Right now, however, she needed to figure a way out of her current predicament. She took a deep breath, held it for a couple of seconds, then slowly expelled it.

She turned toward the man seated next to her, the man piloting the helicopter. Everything had happened so quickly she had not even gotten a good look at him. One moment she had been on her backside in a snowdrift on a country road, desperately trying to get her car unstuck, and the next moment she found herself slung over this stranger's shoulder like a sack of flour as he ran toward the waiting helicopter. She had been aware that he was tall, an inch or two above six feet, but everything else was just a blurred impression of a man wearing dark glasses and bundled up in a heavy jacket.

She finally managed to utter a few words, the first attempt at any conversation on either of their parts. "Who are you? Where are you taking me?"

He did not respond to her questions. The loud noise of the engine and the rotor blade drowned out her words and made conversation impossible. She studied him as they flew toward what she assumed would be a small local airport, someplace where she could get help with her car and hopefully find a motel where she could spend the night.

His blond hair was thick and a little long, but it seemed to suit his strong, chiseled features—at least the ones she could see with his jacket collar turned up around his neck and cheeks. His dark glasses prevented her from seeing the color of his eyes. His face was tanned, and his skin seemed to be showing the first signs of the effect of working outdoors in adverse weather conditions. She guessed his age to be mid to late thirties. The way this ruggedly handsome man had picked her up in one easy move and thrown her over his shoulder said he had to be in superb physical condition.

A few minutes later a large ranch house, barn, stables, corral and a cluster of surrounding structures came into sight. Snow had already started falling again when the helicopter touched down next to one of the small buildings. The stranger jumped out of the helicopter and was met by two men who ran from the barn. "See that the copter's secured real tight, Ben. We're in for a bad one."

The older of the two men took charge. "I was getting worried about you, Jace. I was afraid the storm was going to cut you off and leave you grounded out in the middle of nowhere. They say the main thrust is going to hit with a vengeance—Arctic blast of freezing temperatures, strong winds, possibly as much as three feet of snow."

"We usually get one pre-season snowstorm, sort of nature's warning that winter is on the way, but nothing like this. I hope it moves on as fast as it came in." Jace turned toward the ranch house, calling back over his shoulder to Samantha. "Come on, let's get inside. You must be nearly frozen."

Before she could respond, he was halfway across the

yard. She ran to catch up with him, her progress anything but graceful as she tried to keep from stumbling while running through the snow buildup. This certainly was not an airport, but at that moment the only thing she wanted was to be somewhere warm and dry. She finally caught up with him at the porch of the ranch house. He held open the front door and she hurried inside. She spotted the fireplace and went straight to it, then kicked off her wet shoes and set them on the hearth. Her feet were almost numb with the cold, and her silk pantsuit was undoubtedly ruined. Her teeth chattered, and her hands trembled as she held them out toward the warmth of the flames. She knew she looked more like a rag doll that had just been run through the washing machine than a successful businesswoman.

She sensed his nearness, as if he were standing immediately behind her. Even with her back to him she could feel his eyes on her. She wanted to attribute the odd sensation that shivered across her nape to the cold, but she knew it was not that simple. She turned around. He stood not more than four feet from her.

He had taken off his dark glasses. She stared up into intelligent silver eyes that peered intently at her, seemingly studying her every move. Something about this imposing stranger reached out and grabbed her as nothing ever had before, and she did not understand it. The odd sensation that slowly spread through her entire body had a downright sensual feel about it. There had to be a rational explanation for what was happening. She was a sensible, logical person. Unfortunately, there was nothing sensible or logical about the very real attraction she felt toward him.

She glanced quickly around the room, then returned her attention to the man who continued to stare at her.

"Who are you? Where am I? Why have you brought me here?" She caught the undertone of apprehension that came out in her voice even though she tried to control it. "This certainly isn't an airport."

"My name's Jace Tremayne and this is my ranch. We're here because the storm was closing in around us and I needed to get home before we were cut off and forced to land in the middle of a pasture." He blatantly looked her up and down. "I think you'd better get out of those clothes."

She felt her eyes widen in shock. Had she understood him correctly? Had he brought her to an isolated ranch just so he could tell her to take off her clothes? She swallowed the nervousness that tried to climb out of her stomach as she took a step backward. "Uh...excuse me?"

"Your clothes...they're wet and you've been out in the cold air. You need to get dry and warm or else you'll end up sick." He pointed down the hallway. "The second door on the right is a guest room with a private bathroom. You might want to take a hot bath, too. It'll help you warm up. You'll find clean towels in the cupboard."

He seemed oblivious to the momentary anxiety his comments had caused her. Perhaps she had read far more into what he said than was really there. The *logical* assumption would be that she had simply overreacted to his specific words due to the uneasiness caused by her sudden and unexpected attraction to him. Yes, that had to be it. She felt a desperate need to bring some type of logical control to what was happening, and felt satisfied with her assessment of the situation. Unfortunately her physical attraction to him did not fit as comfortably as her rationalization did.

His comment about her wet clothes had been correct, though. "That's...uh...very generous of you, lending me your guest room."

The first thing Jace had noticed about her was that her clothing wasn't suited to cattle country and was totally inappropriate for the weather. There was no question that she was completely out of her element. There was also no question that despite her disarray she was a pleasure to look at. He was even willing to admit that she was beautiful, an honest beauty that reached out and grabbed him.

He could also admit that he found her an incredibly desirable woman, *if* he were willing to be that honest with himself. He shoved the thoughts aside. He did not have time for idle speculation of a personal nature. Besides, the direction of those thoughts made him decidedly uncomfortable.

"I certainly appreciate the offer of a hot bath, but I don't have any dry clothes to put on. My suitcase is still in the trunk of my car." She wasn't sure whether to be angry with him for literally abducting her without even one word of explanation or grateful to him for rescuing her from what was obviously a bad situation. She tried to suppress her irritation. "You grabbed me and forced me into your helicopter so quickly that I didn't have an opportunity to get it."

"You were obviously in trouble, so I did what needed to be done. There wasn't time to debate the issue."

Her moment of concern no longer seemed appropriate. She did not sense any feeling of personal danger, at least not physical danger.

"Wait here." Jace turned and walked away. Now she really didn't know what to do or think. A couple of minutes later he returned and handed her a thick terry cloth bathrobe. "Here, you can put this on until your clothes dry." She accepted it, folding it across her arm.

A stern look crossed his face, and his voice took on a hard edge. "I have lots to do before the brunt of this storm hits, but when I get back you can tell me what the hell you were doing driving around the back roads in a snowstorm dressed like you were going to some uptown art gallery. Didn't you even bother to listen to a weather forecast before you took your leisurely drive through the countryside with your common sense stuck up your CD player? You're lucky I spotted you, otherwise you'd be in real serious trouble."

"What?" His unexpected—and what she considered unfounded—verbal attack slapped across her senses and brought out her defensive anger. "I was hardly taking a leisurely afternoon drive in the country. I—" If the truth were known, that was pretty much what she had been doing. She had been mindlessly and blindly driving without any thought to where she was going and no purpose to her actions. She was not even sure when or why she had decided to get off the interstate. She had been totally oblivious to her surroundings. It was something she had never done before and was not about to admit to this very disconcerting stranger.

He stood tall with his arms folded across the front of his heavy jacket. He cocked his head and raised an eyebrow, but maintained his stern expression. "You were...what?"

She rubbed her hand across the back of her neck as she tried to calm her inner jitters. "I...I had gotten lost. I was disoriented by the storm and was trying to find my way back to the main highway."

He displayed a smug *why am I not surprised* expres-

sion that carried over into his tone of voice. "Humph!
Just like a woman—no sense of direction."

Her temper flared. "Exactly what do you mean by
'just like a woman'? What are you, one of those chauvinistic types who think the womenfolk should stick to
the cleaning and cooking and not try to do anything
complicated like compete in the world of big business
because that's *men's* work?"

He blatantly looked her up and down again. "I can
only go by what I see standing in front of me...a woman
dressed in a silk suit with fancy shoes and a lightweight
jacket in the middle of a snowstorm who doesn't even
know where she is."

She felt herself losing the battle, but had to give it
one last try. "I knew where I was before you grabbed
me off the road and took me somewhere in a helicopter.
You didn't even bother to ask me if I needed help. You
simply took it upon yourself to decide that you knew
best!"

"I thought you just said you were lost and trying to
find your way back to the main highway." Again the
smug look covered his features. "I guess I must have
misunderstood you. So, just where were you headed
when your superb sense of direction put you on a country road and buried you in the snow?"

"I don't think it's any of your business!" As soon as
the words were out of her mouth, she knew she should
not have said them. They sounded too harsh, too defensive. They also sounded downright rude and very ungrateful. After all, she had been stranded on a back road
and stuck in the snow. She should be thanking him for
saving her, not being antagonistic.

She glanced down at the floor, took a calming breath,
then recaptured his gaze. "Look...I'm sorry. I didn't

mean to snap at you like that. This whole thing has been a very unnerving experience for me. I'm not accustomed to dealing with chaos and disorder. I don't like being forced into making snap decisions. I prefer to have things carefully planned out. I had been visiting...uh...a friend and...well, things didn't—''

She felt the shiver across her nape. Again she was certain that it had nothing to do with being wet and cold. Everything about this Jace Tremayne—his words, his decisive actions, even his body language—said he was a very dynamic man. Overbearing, arrogant and chauvinistic, but very dynamic. He also radiated a tantalizing sex appeal that he did not seem to even be aware of.

His attitude softened a little bit. "Do you need to call anyone to let them know you're all right? Any family members who might be worried?'' He hesitated for a moment before continuing. "The friend you were visiting...or perhaps your husband?''

A couple of days ago she would have called Jerry Kensington. But now... "No, there's no one I need to call.'' She tried to shake away the sudden feeling of despair that threatened to overwhelm her. She looked up at him. Once again his silver eyes seemed to be attempting to penetrate through to her inner soul. She glanced down at the floor, unable to hold his gaze any longer for fear he could read her every thought and feeling.

He pointed down the hallway, once again indicating the guest room. "The second door on the right.''

Samantha opened her mouth to speak, but his actions stopped her words when he turned and walked out the front door. Just what had she gotten herself into? She certainly had not made any provisions for this strange turn of events when she had originally formulated her travel plans. A cold shiver darted through her body, reminding her of her wet clothes and need of a hot bath.

She carried the robe with her as she headed toward the guest room, pausing for a moment to look out a window. Large snowflakes filled the air and the wind had picked up considerably. She saw Jace disappear across the yard toward the barn. She pursed her lips, and a slight frown wrinkled across her brow as she turned away from the window. He had certainly pulled her out of a very precarious situation, but had he deposited her into an even more perilous one?

She was acutely aware of the totally out-of-character thoughts and feelings he stirred in her. She found him aggravating, he and his snap decisions made without benefit of proper thought and planning. But there was more, much more. She was far from being a prude, but the way he made her insides quiver with excitement was something beyond her logical reasoning. She had certainly never experienced that same type of excitement with Jerry Kensington. She glanced out the window again.

The whole idea was preposterous. Jace Tremayne was in no way representative of what her ideal man should be: a professional man; someone who carefully scheduled his activities; someone whose life was planned out and knew what he would be doing five years from now; someone who thrived on the stimulation provided by city life. In short, nothing like what she had observed of Jace Tremayne.

While his unexpected guest thawed out, Jace had several duties to handle. So why was he standing in the barn staring back at the house and making no effort to move? He did not know where this woman had come from or why she had been out on the road. He did not even know her name.

He did know that she was argumentative, stubborn and overly opinionated. He also knew she was hiding something. He could see it in her eyes, in the way certain things made her nervous. She was a strong and assertive woman, yet he sensed a vulnerability—a carefully hidden side that she tried not to show. He was also aware that she possessed the very real ability to slice right through to the center of his most heated desires, seemingly without even being aware of it. The realization left him decidedly unnerved.

He relaxed his tensed nerves and allowed a slight grin to tug at the corners of his mouth. Her angry accusation about him being a chauvinist, who thought a woman's place was cooking and cleaning, amused him. His wife had been a creative, independent woman. They had met when she'd marched up to his front door and informed him that she was researching a book about the history of Wyoming and it would not be complete without information about his family, since they figured prominently. He'd told her there was plenty of information in the University library, but she had refused to take no for an answer.

Her death had hit him very hard. His own life had been so empty for the past four years. Work had kept him busy, but it hadn't erased the hollow feeling that had lived inside him from the day his wife of only two years died of injuries incurred in an automobile accident. She had been three months pregnant with their first child. To compensate for the loss, he'd thrown himself into the needs of the ranch, putting in long hard hours. His unceasing efforts had paid off with material rewards, but his deepest emotions had remained locked away where they could not be trampled on again.

Then one stormy day this woman appeared from out of nowhere and intruded into his life. Even though their meeting was abrupt, the circumstances unusual and their contact best described as adversarial, she had certainly managed to arouse his long-dormant libido. For the first time in four years he felt a strong physical attraction to a woman—a woman he knew was totally wrong for him.

He allowed a slight furrow of his brow as he glanced down at the ground. It bothered him that she did not have anyone to call, that there was no one who would be worried about her. The hurt that had shown in her eyes also bothered him. Perhaps she, too, had suffered a very personal tragedy in her life, just as he had.

"The copter's tied down. Should be okay."

Jace shifted his attention to the medium-sized man in his early forties who had just come in the side door of the barn. Ben Downey was his ranch foreman. Jace was thankful for the interruption that put a halt to his thoughts about his very attractive houseguest, the ones that were starting to turn decidedly personal. "Good…thanks. Why don't you check here in the barn to make sure everything is securely fastened, and I'll make another pass through the stables. Have one of the boys pile extra firewood in the bins at the bunkhouse and ranch house. Have Vince check the emergency generator, make sure it's ready to go on-line. It could be days before this storm clears. If it's bad enough, the power lines could snap again like they did three years ago."

Samantha emerged from the guest room an hour later, half that time having been spent soaking in a hot bath and trying her best not to think about the sensual thrill that tingled through her body whenever Jace Tremayne drew close to her. She had to keep telling herself that she would be leaving his ranch very soon, and the physical excitement he stirred in her would thankfully be put to rest.

She snuggled inside the bathrobe he had given her, having left her damp clothes hanging in the bathroom to finish drying. The robe belonged to a woman, but was at least three sizes too large for her. The texture of the terry cloth against her bare skin heightened her awareness of her nudity beneath the robe. She tightened the sash around her waist, then padded barefoot down the carpeted hallway to the living room seeking out the added warmth of the fireplace.

It was the first time she had relaxed since getting off the plane in Denver and driving to her fiancé's house. She had been engaged to Jerry Kensington for almost a year, even though they lived a thousand miles apart. She had insisted on a two-year engagement. She believed that was the sensible and logical thing to do. It would give them a proper amount of time to discover any possible difficulties in their relationship, and plan out their future.

The past two months, however, had been difficult ones for her. In spite of all her careful planning, she'd had the feeling that something was wrong. What bothered her the most was that she did not feel as upset about that possibility as she should have. She had refused to deal with the fact that perhaps she did not love Jerry, at least not enough to sustain a marriage commitment.

Her trip to Denver was as much to clarify her own feelings as to see Jerry. He continually chided her about being too structured and compulsive, about having to

plan out every facet of her life. She had eagerly anticipated his look of surprise followed by exclamations of
pleasure at her impulsive decision to make the trip.

The image of what had really occurred came rushing
back to her. The shocked expression that had covered
Jerry's face when he opened his front door had not been
one of pleasure. His dark hair was bedroom tousled and
he wore a hastily thrown-on robe. He had stammered
awkwardly while blocking her entrance to the house.
Then she had seen the reason why. The woman who had
casually strolled out of his bedroom was dressed in one
of his T-shirts. It was barely long enough to reach her
upper thighs and she obviously had nothing on underneath it.

Samantha had seen the guilt in his eyes, but his embarrassment had clearly come from having been caught,
rather than any regrets about his actions. She had turned
and walked away, and Jerry Kensington had made no
attempt to stop her. She had never in her life felt as
betrayed as she had at that moment…or as alone.

That was two days ago. Since then she had driven
aimlessly through Colorado and into Wyoming until she
had become stranded in the middle of nowhere, plucked
out of a snowstorm by a stranger in a helicopter and
whisked away to a ranch. She had no idea where she
was, other than somewhere in Wyoming. Her life had
always been so organized, structured and carefully controlled. She had no practical experience dealing with turmoil or unplanned events.

She also had no practical experience with the way
Jace made her feel. The physical side of her relationship
with Jerry Kensington had been carefully planned,
too…just the type of predictability she thought she had
wanted. But it was also dull. Somewhere in the recesses

of her mind she had wished he would just once do something exciting to surprise her. She knew that was an absolute contradiction to everything she had professed to want out of life, but she couldn't stop the thought.

She carefully took in her current surroundings. It was a large, comfortable room that gave the impression of many happy family gatherings over the years. She felt a moment of sadness. Happy family gatherings had not been part of her childhood. And now, after that disastrous and humiliating scene with her fiancé—she corrected herself: Jerry Kensington was now her *ex*-fiancé—it did not look as though they would be part of her future, either.

She straightened her posture and squared her shoulders as she forced a new determination. It was obvious that being in a relationship—marriage and a family—was not to be. She would throw herself into her career and concentrate on being a success in the business world. It would guarantee her a comfortable future. That should be enough. Being stuck at this ranch was only a minor interruption of her plan. She would make the best of it for the short duration of her stay, then return to Los Angeles as soon as the weather cleared.

A cold blast of air whipped in as Jace came through the front door. He stomped his boots on the floor mat to knock away the snow, pulled off his gloves and removed his heavy jacket. Then his gaze fell on the mystery lady. There was something very appealing about the way the large robe enclosed her body—and very enticing. He cleared his mind of the inappropriate thoughts and crossed the room to the fireplace. "Did you find everything you need?"

"Yes, thank you." She turned up the collar of the robe, then nervously tugged at the sash, pulling it tighter around her waist. "I sure appreciate the use of this robe." His nearness sent little tingles across her bare skin and a flush of heat across her cheeks. She lowered her gaze to the floor, too embarrassed to meet the silvery shimmer of his eyes any longer. She tried to calm the nervous excitement that welled inside her.

"The robe belongs to Helen. I'll pass on your appreciation." He could not stop the surge of desire that rushed through him.

Her voice quavered slightly, attesting to a nervousness. "Helen? Who is she?"

He paid an undue amount of attention to the fire in an effort to dismiss the very real physical allure that continued to tug at his consciousness. "Helen Downey. She's the housekeeper and cook. Her son, Ben, is my ranch foreman."

Samantha looked around, searching for the owner of the robe. "Is she here? I'd like to thank her for the considerate gesture."

"Nope. Helen's in Florida visiting her daughter." Jace stared at his houseguest for an uncomfortable moment. She smelled of soap and radiated a scrubbed freshness. She stood about five foot six. Her short, chestnut-colored hair feathered softly around her face, accentuating her delicate features. Her neatly pedicured toes peeked out from beneath the long robe.

Another hard jolt of desire stabbed at his insides, then reverberated through his body. He did not even know her name. He had not asked, and she had not volunteered the information. It made the whole thing seem strangely exciting, almost like some sort of clandestine rendezvous designed strictly for lascivious pleasure without any strings or emotional attachments.

His disconcerting stare caused little tremors to form

inside her body. She took a calming breath and tried her best to project a businesslike outer persona while attempting to regain control of the situation. "I'm afraid we sort of got off on the wrong foot. I've been very inconsiderate in not introducing myself. My name is Samantha Burkett and I'm from Los Angeles." She held out her hand toward him. "And you said you're Jace Tremayne?" The moment their hands clasped together she felt the outdoors cold that lingered on his skin. But underneath that exterior was a very human warmth that radiated a soft glow and sent a sensual little tingle up her arm.

"Tremayne..." He had not released her hand from his grasp nor had she withdrawn it. "I remember seeing a large gated entrance with the name Tremayne above it, and I think Tremayne Road was where I had turned just before skidding into that snowdrift. Is that you?"

"That was my great-great-grandfather. He settled on this land and started the ranch shortly after the Union Pacific Railroad was established here, several years before Wyoming was even a state. The ranch's primary business has always been the raising of beef cattle, but my father expanded into other areas when he granted some mining leases on the northern acreage about twenty-five years ago."

"I've always lived in a large city, and I don't really know anything about ranching. In fact, I've never even been on a ranch before, or a farm, either. It would seem to me to be an isolated type of lifestyle. How far are you from a real city?"

The warmth lingered even after he withdrew his hand, but the soft glow quickly disappeared as his eyes narrowed before he responded to her question. "A *real* city? As opposed to what? Oh, yes. You're from Los

Angeles...obviously a *real* city. However, your car had
Colorado license plates.''

She caught the edge of sarcasm in his voice. His statement sounded more like an accusation than a comment.
"It's a rental from the Denver airport. I picked it up a
couple of days ago.''

Jace cocked his head, a quizzical expression spreading
across his face. "You flew from Los Angeles to Denver,
rented a car and then drove out into a snowstorm dressed
in a silk suit? Do you always set out on such harebrained
and foolhardy escapades?''

He may have been a momentary knight in shining
armor whose charging white steed was really a helicopter, but that did not give him the right to pry into her
personal life. She made no effort to hide her irritation.
"I'm not an irrational person, and I've never done an
impulsive thing in my—'' Well, she couldn't say that
anymore. It was her one and only impulsive action that
had gotten her into this mess.

She nervously played with the gold chain around her
neck. "I'm a professional businesswoman and am accustomed to dressing in a businesslike manner.''

The hint of sarcasm she had noticed earlier in his
voice had intensified. "Oh? And just what is it you do
in that professional businesswoman capacity of yours
while living in a *real* city?''

He seemed to be baiting her, and she did not understand why. "I work for a consulting firm. I do time-and-
motion studies for large corporations to help them run
their operations more efficiently.''

He could not stop his total surprise from coming
through. "You're an efficiency expert?'' He quickly regained his composure. "Then you should have done a
more efficient job of planning your trip.'' He wasn't sure

why he had taken such a harsh attitude with her. It was not his nature to be sarcastic or argumentative. There was something very disconcerting about this woman, something that aroused his most basic desires, and it made him uncomfortable. He tried to alleviate his concerns by reminding himself that she was just passing through and would be leaving as soon as possible to return to the *real* city—a place that apparently suited her lifestyle.

She glared at him. "I might have acted foolishly, even a bit impetuously, but that doesn't make me an empty-headed ditz, and I'd appreciate it if you would remember that!" She stood with her hands on her hips, making an obvious effort to look as tough as possible. "I certainly owe you my gratitude for pulling me out of a difficult situation, but I resent your insinuation that I've got a screw loose!"

Two

Jace could not stop the smile from spreading across his face, then he broke out into an uninhibited laugh that filled the room with warmth and fun. Maybe it was the way she stood glaring at him, trying her best to be all hard edges and cold steel, when in fact she was soft curves and warm flesh.

Samantha blinked a couple of times, then stared at him in disbelief. "What do you find so funny, Mr. Tremayne?"

"It's Jace. Please...call me Jace."

His smile was so infectious that her anger drained away, leaving her feeling a little foolish...and confused. "All right...Jace." She wasn't sure what to say or how to proceed. She returned a somewhat shy smile, then glanced around the room again. "This is a nice house. Has it been here from the time of your great-great-grandfather?"

"The central core of the house, this room and three others, are about 120 years old. There have been several additions and upgrades over the years, resulting in this large, rambling structure."

"I live in a small apartment." She looked up at him. Her gaze locked with his. She experienced a shortness of breath and her words became hesitant. "It...it must be very nice to have so much room for you and your family." It had been an innocent statement on her part. She hadn't consciously given any thought as to whether Jace Tremayne was married.

No—that was certainly not true. She had noticed as soon as he had removed his gloves that he wore no wedding ring. She'd also been aware of the lack of *family* things in the house. There were old photographs of people she assumed to be family members, but nothing to indicate a wife and children. And then there was the robe. It belonged to his housekeeper, not his wife.

Jace nervously shifted his weight from one foot to the other. "I...uh...my family doesn't live here. There is the full-time ranch staff, of course. And Helen...and Ben. My parents...the winters got to be too much for them...and, uh...well, they live in Scottsdale, Arizona." What was there about Samantha Burkett that caused him to suddenly start stammering like some sort of adolescent schoolboy? He felt the irritation spreading inside him. He had never had that problem before and he did not like the feeling.

"I think the fire could use some more wood." It was a minor diversion, but one he desperately needed. He grabbed a couple of logs and added them in the fireplace.

He turned back to face Samantha. He felt awkward asking the question of a total stranger, especially considering the very real physical desire that had been constantly tugging at his consciousness ever since her arrival, but reality had to be dealt with and the storm outside was the reality of the moment. "You do know that you'll have to stay here overnight, don't you? Maybe even longer."

Jace saw the objection forming on her face and the uncertainty in her hazel eyes that quickly changed to concern as she took a step backward. He spoke in a very matter-of-fact tone. "No point in you accepting or rejecting the idea. It's out of your hands...and out of my hands, too. The weather dictates. Right now all but the main highway is shut down and it looks like that could be shut down, at any time. With the winds kicking up the way they are, taking the copter up is not an option."

A sudden jolt of apprehension hit Samantha. She didn't want it to sound as if she were accusing him of improper behavior, but she wasn't sure how she felt about staying overnight in a house alone with him, especially in light of the unexpected attraction she felt toward him. "You...uh...said your housekeeper, Helen, is visiting her daughter in Florida? Are you the only ones who live in this house? I mean, it's such a large house for only two people. Don't any of the other employees...." She was not sure how to finish her sentence.

"The ranch hands live in the bunkhouse. It's not as austere as it sounds. Unlike the picture presented in the movies and on television, it's actually more akin to a college dorm. There are bedrooms with two people to a room, plus a central living-dining room and a kitchen. It's really quite comfortable."

"Well, that's certainly different from what I would have thought." The anxiety still flitted around inside her stomach. It looked as if it would be just the two of them in the house after all.

"You seem to be uncomfortable," Jace said. "Let me assure you that you're perfectly safe—"

"Oh, no…it's not that. I certainly didn't mean to imply—" Embarrassment cut off her words as she turned back toward the fire. She didn't have a problem talking with people, even complete strangers. Being able to communicate information was part of her job. So why was she having so much difficulty talking with Jace Tremayne? And exactly what was her problem? Perhaps her concerns were not with Jace's behavior, but rather with her own desires and curiosities about this incredibly sexy man.

Samantha stared at the flames in the fireplace. She'd been totally unprepared for any of the happenings that had occurred since she left Los Angeles. Spur-of-the-moment decisions and snap judgments were not part of her life. She needed to plan, to research, to gather all the facts and study all available information in order to make an intelligent evaluation and determine a viable procedure. The last few days had presented her with enough unexpected happenings to fill her quota for several years.

And the biggest surprise of all was the way Jace Tremayne made her insides quiver and her pulse race. It was inappropriate, very confusing…and very real. It was also totally absurd. He was a cowboy, a rugged outdoors man—not at all the type of man who would fit into her world. And a cattle ranch in Wyoming was certainly no place for her.

She shoved away the inappropriate thoughts. She was not sure where they had come from, but she wished they would go away. She had nothing in common with him, and that was the end of it.

The front door flew open with a loud crash, sending

a blast of cold air through the room. Samantha and Jace both turned to see what was going on.

"I think we're okay, Jace." Ben Downey quickly closed the door. He removed his hat and hit it against his leg to knock off the snow, then stomped his boots against the floor mat before venturing into the room. "Denny and George are going to do periodic checks of the barn and henhouse. If the storm cuts off the electricity, we'll need to get generator power to those incubators as soon as possible or we'll lose all the chicks." Ben paused as he stared at Samantha.

Jace quickly made the introductions. "Ben, this is Samantha Burkett. Her car was stuck in the snow. I spotted her just as I made the final pass over the back pasture before heading home. It looks like she'll be staying here until things clear out. Samantha, this is Ben Downey, my ranch foreman."

Ben nodded toward Samantha. "Pleased to meet you, ma'am. Sorry about the storm putting a hitch in your plans." Ben returned his attention to Jace and the business at hand. "I need to get some extra supplies transferred from the pantry to the bunkhouse kitchen." Ben hurried out the door to complete his chores, once again braving the stormy afternoon.

Jace had been thankful for the break in his conversation with Samantha. Her apparent concerns were groundless. Of course she was safe in the house alone with him. But that didn't mean that a delicious fantasy had not crossed his mind. He hadn't dated since his wife's death, nor had he wanted to. He'd finally settled comfortably into a moderately content day-to-day existence. It was not exciting, but then he hadn't met anyone who excited him...not until now.

As improbable as it seemed, Samantha was definitely

that someone. By her own admission she had never been on a ranch and knew nothing of rural life. Her world was silk suits and the big city. So what was there about her that he found so irresistible? Why did he want to take her into his arms and make love to her until they were both too exhausted to move?

It was no good. He needed to elevate his thoughts higher than his belt buckle and move the conversation to safer ground. "I suppose the next order of business is to give you a tour of the house." Jace waved his arm to encompass all the surrounding area. "This, as you've seen, is the living room." He took her through the dining room, kitchen, den, and finally gestured down the hallway toward the bedrooms. They returned to the living room.

"It's a very comfortable house. You can tell it's had many years of love and care," Samantha said, her sadness working its way to the surface.

She had never lived in a loving home. She had worked hard her entire life in an attempt to make her parents proud of her. No matter how hard she tried, or how much she accomplished, she was never able to elicit even one word of praise from them. She had thought a good marriage might please them. Jerry Kensington had all the credentials they could have wanted—a good family background, a Harvard education, and a successful law practice.

The thought slapped her across the face, startling her with the clarity of the realization. Had that been the only reason she had become engaged to Jerry? Yet another attempt to garner some spark of approval from her parents? Was it possible that she'd never really loved him at all? And then the ultimate question—had she nearly ruined her life by entering a loveless marriage simply to please her parents? It was a very disturbing thought and only went to reinforce her earlier determination—marriage might be all right for other people, but it was not for her. A serious relationship would only get in the way of her career.

She returned her attention to Jace, who glanced at the clock on the mantel. "Make yourself at home. I would imagine you're probably hungry. Help yourself to whatever you'd like in the kitchen." He reached for his gloves and heavy jacket. "There's television and plenty of reading material in the den. I've still got a few more hatches to batten down before the day is over." Before she could reply, he disappeared through the front door.

Hungry. Yes, she certainly was that. It was past three o'clock in the afternoon, and she hadn't eaten anything since toast, juice and coffee that morning. She also needed to do something about clothes. Her thoughts, and the realization of her physical attraction toward Jace, had made her doubly aware of the fact that she had nothing on beneath the robe he had given her to wear. Her silk suit was already ruined, so tossing it in a clothes dryer with her panties and bra couldn't possibly do it any more harm.

She located the utility room, put her clothes in the dryer, then wandered back to the kitchen. She opened the refrigerator door and stared at the contents. Everything seemed to need some sort of preparation, unlike her own kitchen where things only required minimal heating if even that. She went to the freezer. Perhaps she'd find a frozen entreé of some kind that she could pop into the microwave. Again, nothing of the sort. Then she noticed there was no microwave.

She gave the kitchen a closer inspection. A six-burner stove, large double ovens, bins of flour and sugar, cupboards of staples, shelves of home-canned fruits and vegetables. There was nothing that suited her extremely limited culinary talents. Since her chances of being able to get a pizza delivered to a ranch house in the middle of a snowstorm were decidedly slim, she settled on making a piece of toast and pouring a glass of milk.

As soon as the dryer shut off, she quickly changed back into her clothes. She had been correct: her pants and blouse were ruined, but at least they gave her something to wear. She paused outside the door as she left the guest room, taking a moment to glance down the hallway. Her curiosity overruled her sense of propriety.

She peeked in the other rooms—an office, two other bedrooms and one more bathroom, in addition to the guest room she was using. None of the rooms revealed any hint of a wife or children.

The room at the end of the hall was a master bedroom with fireplace and private bath. The unmade bed, coupled with the pair of jeans and denim shirt draped across the arm of a chair told her the room belonged to Jace. She glanced back toward the front door, then entered his bedroom.

The room itself seemed very comfortable, though it was sparsely decorated with large areas where things should have been but were not, as if they had been removed without being replaced. She hesitantly reached out and touched the bed, then ran her hand across the indentation in one of the pillows. A hot jolt of pure lust shot up her arm. She quickly turned and left the room.

She went to the den in search of a good book to pass the time...and take her mind off the sensual feel of Jace's bed and the desires it stirred. She paused at a window. The storm had cut off most of the daylight, giving the scene a bleak appearance. Snow blanketed

everything and continued to fall without sign of letup.
The strong wind plastered it against the side of the house
and whipped it into large drifts across the yard. She shivered as she watched the intensity increase with each
passing minute.

Two men leaned into the wind as they made their way
across the yard, their image obscured by the blowing
snow. One of them turned toward the barn and the other
turned toward the house. A moment later she heard
someone enter through the front door. She returned her
attention to the bookshelves lining the walls.

Jace stomped the snow from his boots and hung his
hat and jacket on the rack by the door. He headed
straight to the fireplace, grabbed a couple more logs and
added them to the fire. Everything possible had been
done to prepare for the duration of what looked to be a
full-scale blizzard. Now it was a matter of attending to
the necessary daily ranch chores and hoping the storm
didn't do damage to any of the buildings.

He checked the kitchen and dining room, but did not
see Samantha. He rubbed his hands in front of the fire
until the chill was gone, then went looking for her. He
spotted her in the den. He leaned against the doorjamb
and watched her for a moment. She stood on her toes
with her arm stretched above her head in an attempt to
reach something. His gaze lingered on the fabric of her
slacks and the way it caressed the roundness of her bottom.

He took a couple of steps into the room, then paused.
He allowed his gaze to travel up to the soft silk that
clung to the curve of her breast. The wrinkled and di-
sheveled condition of her clothes could not hide the enticing sight that made his blood course a little faster. He
closed his eyes for a moment. He knew he could not

continue to stare at her as if she were a hot meal and he hadn't eaten in four years—regardless of how much his gaze wanted to linger.

He crossed the den and stood behind her. "Let me help you."

"Oh!" She glanced over her shoulder and lowered her arm. "You startled me. I didn't hear you come into the room."

"What is it you're trying to reach?"

She turned back toward the books and extended her arm, pointing to the object of her interest. "I was trying to get that book." A tremor of delight suffused her body when she felt him brush against her back and shoulder.

He reached past her and grabbed the tome from the shelf. He felt her warmth, an almost seductive heat that grabbed hold of him and refused to let go. He took a steadying breath as he tried to regain control. He had difficulty getting out the words. "Is there anything else you wanted?"

"No...nothing else." She turned to face him and found herself so close that their bodies almost touched. His silver eyes captured her just as surely as if he had wrapped her in his embrace. She felt the very real pull of his magnetic sexuality. It nearly took her breath away. No one had ever made her feel that way before, certainly not her ex-fiancé.

He handed her the book, then quickly took a step backward.

Her words were almost a whisper. "Thank you."

His gaze fell on her mouth for a moment. Her lips slowly parted. Her lower lip quivered slightly as she ran the tip of her tongue across her upper lip in a nervous manner. He swallowed hard, then took another calming breath in an attempt to find some composure. "I'm sorry to have left you on your own like this, but a storm of this magnitude requires extra work. Snow is not uncommon, but a raging blizzard this time of year is unusual. We don't usually get hit this hard until after Christmas. We could be in for a few rough days.''

She followed his lead by engaging in idle chitchat in an attempt to impose some control on what was happening. ''I understand perfectly. I certainly don't want to be a bother to you. I know you have lots to do.'' She felt a shortness of breath caused by his close proximity. She had such a tenuous hold on her soaring desires, and the totally unfamiliar state left her feeling very uncomfortable.

She clutched the book tightly in her hand. The way he continued to look at her did not help matters at all. ''I...uh.'' She nervously played with the gold chain around her neck. ''I just realized that I never properly thanked you for your timely rescue. Everything happened so quickly. My car skidded into a snowdrift, then your helicopter swooped down out of the sky. The next thing I knew I was standing in your living room. I guess it took me a while to catch up with all of it.''

She awkwardly shifted her weight from one foot to the other. ''When I looked out the window a few minutes ago and saw the way the snow was coming down and the wind blowing, I realized just how much trouble I would have been in if you hadn't come along. And your hospitality—'' She could not handle being this close to him. She put some more space between them. ''I want to do something to repay your kindness.'' She wasn't sure what else to say. ''Maybe I could pay for my room and meals...''

Jace experienced a pang of disappointment at the turn of events, but he was glad that she'd decided to put more distance between them. He had been very tempted to pull her into his arms and kiss that very alluring mouth. It was a temptation that had been growing stronger and stronger despite the fact that he didn't want it to be so.

He quickly recovered and addressed her last comment, just a hint of irritation creeping into his voice. "You want to pay me for your room and meals? This isn't a boarding house. I guess things are different in Los Angeles and other *real* cities. This is ranch country. Neighbors help out neighbors. Quite often we are dependent on each other, especially in emergency situations like now. That same courtesy extends to strangers in need, too."

The shocked look on her face made him regret the words as soon as they were out of his mouth. It wasn't like him. He was not an argumentative type of person. There was just something about Samantha Burkett that seemed to make him say things totally out of character. It was almost as if he were trying to build a wall between them for fear it would prove much too tempting if he allowed her to get too close.

In the four years since his wife's death he'd managed to drag himself up from the depths of despair and get on with his life. The first two years had been very difficult, but the past two years had settled into a normal routine that he was able to live with. He'd pretty much resigned himself to the fact that he would never find another special woman who could be part of his life.

One thing was for certain, he was not ready to expose that fragile place that he'd so carefully hidden away. And even if he did eventually take a chance on exposing those emotions, it would not be with someone as totally unsuited as Samantha Burkett. They were from two different worlds and obviously had nothing in common in spite of the fact that she managed to fan the nearly dead embers of his desires into flames.

Samantha was totally taken aback by his abrupt change in attitude. "I...I'm sorry. I didn't mean to offend you. I'm accustomed to taking care of myself and paying my own way without depending on others. I didn't want you to think I was a freeloader. Perhaps there's something I could do to help out."

"Well...I am a little shorthanded with Helen gone. Maybe you could fill in on some of her chores." It wasn't that he actually needed her help, but he thought it might give her something to do to occupy her time until the storm lifted. Then she would be on her way. As abruptly as she'd appeared, she would just as quickly be gone. They'd remain two people totally unsuited for each other, whose paths happened to momentarily cross one stormy day. Nothing more.

"Uh...yes, of course." She glanced down at the floor, then recaptured his gaze and extended her best professional smile. "I'm not sure how much of a help I'll be, but I'm certainly willing to try. In fact, why don't I start right now by making some coffee? I'm sure this type of cold day calls for something hot to drink, especially after working outside the way you have been."

"While you're doing that, I'm going to put on some dry clothes." Jace hurried down the hall to his bedroom, closed the door, then leaned back against it. He expelled a long, slow breath. A line from the movie *Casablanca* immediately leaped to mind. He changed it slightly to fit his own personal inner turmoil. *Of all the back roads in the county, why did she have to get stuck on mine?*

Samantha carried the book to the guest room and placed it on the night stand. She would read it later. Right now she had other things to do. In the kitchen—

certainly not her favorite room and not where she displayed her greatest proficiency. She squared her shoulders, clenched her jaw and marched determinedly down the hall and through the living room. She repeated the words over and over in her mind, *I can do this...I can do this.*

She carefully measured out the proper amount of coffee from the canister, then added the water and turned on the coffeepot. Next she set out two cups and saucers. She found a sugar bowl, then poured some milk into a cream pitcher. She arranged everything on the table, along with napkins and a spoon next to his coffee cup. She didn't know if he took cream or sugar in his coffee, but she wanted to make sure she was prepared for the eventuality. She stood back and surveyed the scene with a critical eye. She knew it was only coffee, but she wanted to make sure she had not forgotten anything.

"Samantha?" Jace's voice came from the living room moments later.

She heard him call her name, and a fraction of a second later the butterflies began to flit around inside her stomach. She took a calming breath, then called out to him. "In the kitchen."

"Did you find everything okay?" He walked directly to the cupboard and took out a mug without even glancing at the table she had so painstakingly prepared. He grabbed the pot and filled the mug. He took one sip of the coffee, held it in his mouth for a moment, then finally swallowed it. He stared into the mug and scrunched his face into a disagreeable frown before looking quizzically at Samantha. "What is this stuff?"

"It's coffee." She didn't have a clue what had prompted his question and strange behavior. "What did you think it was?"

He dumped the contents of the mug, picked up the pot and poured the rest of the coffee down the drain.

She rushed to the sink, watched the coffee swirl down the drain, then stared up at him. Her bewilderment carried over into the tone of her voice. "What's wrong? What do you think you're doing?"

He threw away the used coffee grounds and started anew. "I'm making coffee. That stuff you made could more aptly be referred to as tea."

"Wait just a minute..." She felt the anger flush across her cheeks. "There was nothing wrong with that coffee. That's the way I always make it and I've never had any complaints before."

"Well, maybe your friends are ultrapolite or maybe they've never had to warm up after being out in a blizzard. Either way, coffee has to be a lot stronger than this barely tinted hot water of yours."

"Strong coffee is not good for the system. Studies show—"

He whirled around to face her. "*Studies* aren't going to warm me up after being outdoors in a subzero wind-chill factor."

She tried to keep the irritation out of her voice, but it crept in anyway. "This falls within the realm of my area of expertise. Studies of the coffee-drinking habits of office workers clearly show—"

His retort was immediate and emphatic. "Running a ranch does not have a parallel connection to working in an office. It's like comparing horses and cattle. They may both be four-legged animals, but that doesn't mean they're interchangeable in their uses."

Her anger flared. She glowered at him as she jumped on what she felt was his unwarranted criticism. "Your horses and cows don't have a thing to do with—"

He moved so quickly that Samantha didn't have time to react. One minute they were engaged in a disagreement that could have turned into a full-scale argument, and the next minute his mouth covered hers with a heated intensity unlike anything she had ever before experienced—a heated intensity that was at the same time strangely hesitant and unsure, a heated intensity that tasted of longing and loneliness as much as desire.

Her first reaction was to pull away from him, even though his attentions were far from being unwanted. It was all so sudden, so startling, so unplanned...and so very exciting. His warmth flowed through her, providing her with a taste of the passion that existed beneath the cool exterior of Jace Tremayne. She lifted her arms around his neck. Then she felt herself being pulled into his embrace.

There was a strength about him that came from the security of knowing who he was and being content with that knowledge. He was a man who knew what he wanted out of life and where he was going. It was the type of strength she had longed for, the type of strength that had eluded her in her drive to please her parents, the type of strength she had not found in the person of Jerry Kensington. It was an honesty she found very appealing...and incredibly sexy.

Three

It would be difficult to say which one broke off the kiss, Jace or Samantha. They seemed to each pull back at the same time. For a long moment they stood together, still entwined in an embrace. The howling wind faded into the background. An almost deafening silence filled the air, broken only by the sound of breathing. Each seemed to be lost in the depths of the other's eyes, looking into the soul in search of...of what? Then reality intruded into the moment and the spell was broken.

Samantha stepped away, coming to an abrupt halt when she backed up against the edge of the kitchen sink. There was no question that the kiss had a very disconcerting effect on her. Her heart pounded. She fought against the shortness of breath that tried to take hold. All the while his silvery-eyed gaze held her as close as his arms had just moments earlier. She didn't know what to say to him about what had just happened. He might have been the one to take her by surprise, but she was every bit as willing a participant as he had been.

She forced her gaze away, glancing out the window at the raging storm. Daylight had faded into gray remnants that would soon be night. The next logical thing would be to fix dinner. That was what she needed to do. She needed to bring a logical order to these unquestionably illogical proceedings. That kiss never happened. It was the best way for her to handle the awkward situation.

"Well…" Her voice cracked as she tried to speak. She cleared her throat and tried again. "It's almost dinnertime."

"Yes, it's almost dinnertime." The huskiness surrounding his words belied his cool and calm exterior. "I have some paperwork to take care of, shouldn't take me more than half an hour. When I'm done, I'll see about getting some dinner on the table."

She immediately jumped in, eager to change the tone of what had been happening. "Let me do it. I can fix dinner while you're taking care of your business."

"You don't need to. Unless you're starving and can't wait, I'll take care of it in a little while."

"Really, I don't mind. I'd like to contribute something." She could feel herself getting in over her head, but she did not seem to be able to stop the words. "I don't mind preparing dinner."

"Well…if you're sure you don't mind." He wanted to get out of the room and away from her. He *needed* to remove himself from her presence before he did something foolish again.

He turned toward the kitchen door. "I'll be in my office if you need me…I mean, if you need anything."

He hurried out of the room without waiting for any response from her.

As much as Jace wanted to take her in his arms again, to taste the sweetness of that delectable mouth, he knew it was out of the question. He also knew that a quick retreat was the only thing that would prevent him from doing just that. He closed his eyes for a moment, allowing the memory of her body pressed against his to wash over him. When he woke that morning, all he'd had to look forward to was extra work preparing for a freak blizzard. It never occurred to him that a simple little thing like pulling a stranded motorist out of the snow could cause him all this inner turmoil, but it had.

He made a decision. The best way for him to handle things was to simply pretend the kiss never happened. He would take care of his paperwork, have dinner, then go to bed early and read for a while. The morning would be a new day, and with any luck the storm would have spent its fury. And when the storm moved on, so would Samantha. She would return to her world and her lifestyle, and he would get on with life. He sat at his desk, turned on the computer and pulled up the file he needed.

In the dining room, Samantha placed the water glasses on the table, then surveyed the setting with a critical eye. What she saw met with her satisfaction. Next she turned her attention to the meal itself. A shudder ran up her back, the sign of apprehension that always appeared whenever she attempted to do something she knew was totally out of her area of expertise. Why in the world had she volunteered to fix dinner of all things? It was stupid for her to have made such an irrational offer, but to have followed it up by insisting…well, it was too late now.

Returning to the kitchen, she opened the refrigerator

and stared at the contents. She was not sure where to begin. A salad. She knew she could handle that without any trouble. She found a nice selection of ingredients— lettuce, tomatoes, mushrooms and bean sprouts. She had also seen some croutons in a cupboard earlier that day. She took a salad bowl from the shelf, then washed the vegetables.

After twenty minutes of careful, conscientious work she had an attractive salad on the table along with formal dinner place settings. She pursed her lips and frowned as she continued to stare. She could be happy with a salad for dinner, but she knew a hardworking rancher would be needing something a lot more substantial than that.

She again stared at the contents of the refrigerator. The only meat she saw that was not frozen was a chicken—a whole chicken that had not been cut into individual pieces. She grabbed the package and set it on the counter. She had never even attempted to cut up a chicken before. She picked up a sharp knife, hesitated a moment, then put it down. She clenched her jaw in determination. For some insane and totally unfathomable reason she had volunteered to fix dinner, and that was what she intended to do. She picked up the knife again.

Jace printed out a report then turned off the computer. He had stalled long enough. There was nothing left for him to do but return to the kitchen. He pushed back from the desk, rose from his chair, took a deep breath and left the room.

He paused at the kitchen door. Samantha had a knife in one hand and a chicken in the other. He wasn't sure exactly what she was trying to accomplish, but whatever it was, she was making a mess of it. If he didn't stop the disaster, there wouldn't be enough of the bird left to serve as dinner for even one person, let alone two people.

Jace crossed the room and took the knife from her, pausing a moment to use the blade to poke at the heap on the cutting board. "What in the world do you think you're doing?" He suppressed a little chuckle. "You've hacked at this poor bird until it's almost unrecognizable."

She looked at her miserable attempt, then back at Jace. To have taken offense at his accusation would have been a waste of time. The evidence was obvious, his statement could not be denied. A hint of embarrassment surrounded her words. "I—I've never had to do this before. The ones in the grocery store are already cut up."

"What were you planning to do with this poor chicken after you finished torturing it?" He noticed that she had selected the wrong type of knife, so he retrieved the proper one from the drawer and expertly separated the thighs from the legs and split the breast in two.

"I—I'm not sure. I guess cook it…somehow. Maybe in…uh…well, there's the oven." She made a feeble gesture toward the stove, then shrugged in a halfhearted manner that said she clearly did not have any sort of a plan in mind. In an attempt to salvage whatever credibility she could, she pointed to the table in the dining room. "I made a salad."

"So I see." He also saw that the table was set for a dinner party, not for dinner. She had made a salad but had nearly destroyed a chicken. He folded his arms across his chest and leveled an appraising look at her while doing his best to hide his amusement.

Samantha steeled herself against Jace's penetrating gaze. She made her living with her communication skills. Her strengths centered on her ability to analyze a problem and pinpoint an efficient and logical solution. However, this one had her stumped. She had nowhere to go and no viable excuse to offer. She had only the truth, as mortifying as it was. She looked at him, squared her shoulders, took a determined breath, then blurted out, "I can't cook. I'm sorry, but that's the way it is." She glanced around the kitchen, then returned her attention to Jace. "Maybe if you had a microwave..."

He stared at her for a moment, disbelief covering his face. "You don't know how to cook?"

"I've never had occasion or the time to learn. I've been too busy, first with school and then with my career." She tried, albeit unsuccessfully, to keep the edge of irritation out of her voice. "The fact that I'm a woman doesn't mean I was born with a fully realized set of domestic skills."

A scowl wrinkled across his face, followed by confusion. "Why are you so angry? If you don't know how to cook, then why did you insist on cooking dinner? I don't understand."

"What?" Had she heard him correctly? "You don't understand? I had agreed to help out in Helen's absence. Perhaps I was a bit too hasty in insisting that I prepare dinner, but I felt I needed to do something—"

"You misunderstood me. When we were talking about you helping out, cooking was *not* what I had in mind."

The same sensation stirred as when he'd told her she needed to get out of her clothes. Could his having initiated the kiss they shared be her answer? She had allowed the kiss, so he assumed she would allow more? She hesitantly tendered her question. "Just what is it you had in mind?"

"The boys in the bunkhouse can fend for themselves

as far as meals are concerned. I'm a fair hand in the kitchen. The help I had in mind was with the daily barnyard chores. You know, things like feeding the chickens, collecting eggs, maybe even milking a cow—"

"Barnyard chores?" Samantha could not stop the shock from covering her face. "I thought...didn't I mention that I'd never been on a ranch before? Or a farm? This," she pointed at the now neatly laid out pieces of chicken, "is the closest I've ever been to a chicken." She saw a hint of something shift through his eyes, then disappear.

"There's no experience required. You take a bucket of feed and throw it around on the ground and the chickens eat it. You reach into the nest, pick up an egg and place it in a basket. Nothing to it."

Disappointment. That was what had darted through his eyes. She was sure of it. She had seen it before, first with her parents, then with Jerry Kensington. She had completely bungled her attempt at fixing dinner, and now she had let him down again. She needed to show him that she was not incompetent. She had agreed to help and she had to honor her word. She needed to prove herself yet again.

"Yes...well, uh...that certainly sounds easy." She assumed a positive attitude in hopes that he would not see her fears and reservations. "I'm sure I can handle that without any problems. When do I start?"

"Tomorrow morning, about five o'clock." He paused for a moment and stared at her, as if turning something over in his mind. A little sigh escaped his throat. "Let's make that six o'clock instead."

Samantha swallowed hard and made a valiant attempt not to register any emotion. "Right, six o'clock. I'll be ready." Six o'clock in the *morning?* She felt the groan rumble up into her throat, but she managed to swallow it before it escaped.

It was obvious that Jace needed to take charge of fixing dinner. They were soon seated at the table enjoying what Samantha had to admit was a surprisingly tasty meal. Jace was more than just "a fair hand" in the kitchen.

"You fixed dinner. I insist on doing dishes," she said and started clearing the table.

Jace gave one final glance toward Samantha's activity, then went to the living room. He grabbed the poker and stoked the fire before adding a couple more logs. The flames erupted with new energy, sending a warm glow through the room. He stared at the fire, momentarily lost in his thoughts. Dinner had been *nice*. He did not know what other word to use. It had been nice. He appreciated Helen's company—after all, she had been at the ranch since he was twelve years old and was just like family. But it had been a long time since he sat across the table from a beautiful, vibrant woman who reminded him that there was a lot more to life than the sterile existence he had been living.

Samantha did more than merely heat up his desires. She also stirred up his thoughts. This self-proclaimed efficiency expert who was so totally out of her element had managed to charm the socks off him without even trying. She was so busy attempting to exert some sort of logical control over things that he doubted she even noticed the way he kept mentally undressing her every time he looked at her.

"The dishes are done and the kitchen is clean."

Jace turned around at the sound of Samantha's voice. He watched as she walked toward him. He read the nervousness and anxiety on her face. He was not sure what had caused it. He hoped it was not any concerns about his behavior or her safety spending the night in the house alone with him. He should never have given in to the urge to kiss her. As much as he had enjoyed it, it was a dumb thing to have done.

"I don't want to be a bother." She glanced down at the floor for a moment before continuing. "At least any more of a bother than I've already been, but I was wondering if…" She nervously shifted her weight from one foot to the other.

"Wondering what? Is there a problem? Something you need?"

"It's my clothes." She tugged at the tail of her wrinkled silk blouse in a subconscious effort to smooth it out. "I'm going to need something warm, and maybe some boots, so I can go out in the snow and cold in the morning to feed the chickens. Do you suppose Helen would have—"

"There's nothing in Helen's closet that would come even close to fitting you."

"Oh." Her disappointment was obvious. "Not even some sort of heavy jacket? It doesn't matter if it's too big, as long as it's warm. I realize this is quite an imposition and I feel so bad about it. I want to help…I promised I'd help you with the chores, but—" She grabbed the bottom of her blouse in one hand to indicate the thinness of the fabric and offered an apologetic shrug.

Jace carefully looked her up and down, not with a sensual eye but rather a critical eye. She appeared to be maybe an inch shorter, but other than that she seemed to be about the same size as his wife. Doubts, confusion and uncertainty flooded over him. He had packed away his pain along with his wife's belongings, locking them in a large trunk for what he assumed would be forever. Did he dare go to the trunk? Open up and unpack the hurt? He was not at all sure it was the best thing to be doing, but it was a solution to the immediate problem. He clenched his jaw, steeling himself for what was to come.

"I think I might be able to find some warm clothes that will fit you." Even to his own ear the words sounded too strained, too uncomfortable. "I—I'll go check on those clothes."

Samantha watched as Jace left the room and headed down the hallway. There was something in his voice, some sort of sadness. She didn't understand where it suddenly came from or why it was there. She stood in front of the fire, closed her eyes and tried once again to bring some kind of order to the chaos that surrounded her. She was stuck somewhere in Wyoming on a ranch in a snowstorm with a complete stranger who had kissed her almost senseless, an endeavor in which she had cooperated fully.

She slowly opened her eyes. The realization was sharp and clear. There was no logic, she had no control...and she didn't know what to do about it. She was temporarily trapped in a place where she would normally never be. And even more absurd was the fact that she found this rancher—this cowboy—incredibly sexy. How was it possible for her entire life to be turned inside out so quickly and so thoroughly? She continued to stare into the flames, not knowing what else to do as she waited for Jace to return.

Jace's hand trembled slightly as he lifted the lid on the old trunk. It had not been opened in four years, not since the day Helen had helped him carefully pack his wife's clothes away along with other personal items that

he could not bear to look at any longer, but could not
bear to part with, either. Was he opening a Pandora's
box only to release all the demons he thought he'd
packed away?

The first thing he saw were the two photographs. One
was their wedding picture and the other was a snapshot
of his wife with her favorite horse. He touched each
photograph, lightly running his fingertips over the surface before picking them up. An odd sensation tingled
across his skin. It was not pain that he found inside the
trunk, it was warm memories of what had been. He did
not exactly understand the feelings, but he embraced
them.

After a moment he selected a couple of pairs of jeans,
a warm pullover sweater, a wool shirt, a winter coat,
some socks and a pair of snow boots. He carefully
placed the photographs back in the trunk with the rest
of the clothes and shut the lid. He took a deep breath,
then slowly exhaled.

A smile curled the corners of his mouth. He pictured
Samantha dressed in the jeans and sweater and wondered
if she could ever become comfortable with the house
and ranch. He quickly rose to his feet and shoved down
the thoughts. No. They were from two different worlds,
and she would be returning to hers as soon as the storm
lifted. That would be the end of it.

He returned to the living room. "I think these will
probably fit you." He handed her the neatly folded
clothing.

She took the items from him while giving him a questioning look that clearly asked where the clothes had
come from. "Thank you. This is very kind of you. It
seems that I keep getting further and further in your debt.
Hopefully this storm will lift tomorrow and I'll be able

to get out of your hair so you can return to a normal routine. I feel bad about causing you all this trouble.'' Yes, she would be returning to what she knew, a place where she was comfortable and functioned efficiently.

Once again their gazes locked for a soul-searching moment. His words were soft as he withdrew his hands, leaving the bundle of clothes with her. ''It's no trouble, no trouble at all.''

Samantha hurried to the guest room to try on the clothes. She was pleased that they fit so well. Even the snow boots were only half a size too large. Wearing two pairs of socks took care of that problem. She returned to the living room to show Jace how well everything fit.

''Well, what do you think?'' She presented herself for his inspection. The unconscious gesture immediately leaped into a conscious thought. She was seeking his approval...just as she had always done with her parents, as she did at work and as she had done with Jerry Kensington. But this stranger had no bearing on her life. Why was it so important for her to have his approval?

''The clothes seem to fit you perfectly.'' He glanced down at her feet and noted she wore socks but no shoes. ''Are the boots going to be okay?''

''Yes, with two pairs of socks they're fine.'' She offered him a sincere smile. ''Thank you very much. It was...uh...fortunate for me that you had these clothes here.''

''They were my wife's.''

Her gaze became riveted to the floor. ''I didn't mean to pry. Please forgive me,'' she said softly.

Jace placed his fingertips beneath her chin and lifted her face until he could look into her eyes. There was such honesty there. He found it every bit as enticing as the taste of her mouth and the texture of her skin.

"There's no reason for you to apologize." His fingertips moved from under her chin until his hand cupped her face. Then he gave in to the temptation of her nearness as his mouth covered hers.

For an hour Samantha had tossed and turned in bed, unable to sleep. She had finally picked up the book she'd taken from the den. It was a history of Wyoming. She read the first chapter, then as she was about to set it aside noticed the dedication. "With love to my husband, Jace. Thank you for your help, moral support and love." She checked the copyright page. The book had been written by Stephanie Tremayne and was published five years ago. His wife? When had they gotten divorced? Somehow that notion did not sit comfortably with her. Why would he still have some of his ex-wife's clothes? Something was out of place.

She closed the book and turned out the light. The numerals on the digital clock glowed red in the dark room—another fifteen minutes and it would be midnight. So many things raced through her mind. It was the same type of anxiety she experienced each time she had a new project at work or had to prove herself to a new client. There were those words again—*prove herself.*

Sleep eluded her and she knew exactly why—Jace Tremayne. She did not know what to make of him. He was a rancher. He lived in a rural world of blue jeans, cattle and horses—far removed from her world of silk suits and the type of city activities she enjoyed.

Twice he had kissed her. The first time she had pretended it had not happened and was fully cognizant that he had done likewise. She thought that would be the end of it. But the second kiss had rocked her right down to her toes. She knew she would not be able to dismiss the hard jolt of physical desire he aroused in her, even though it could not lead to anything more than a passing liaison at best.

She shivered beneath the blankets. She tried to blame her physical sensations on the storm. She knew it was only half the truth. The other half was just down the hall behind a closed door.

Four

Every time Jace closed his eyes he became enmeshed in a sensual fantasy that continued on from where the very real kiss had ended. He and Samantha clearly came from two different worlds and had nothing in common. He loved the ranch and the outdoor life. He found the cold, snowy winters invigorating. Large cities and traffic congestion made him uncomfortable. Yet Samantha stirred physical desires in him that he could not dismiss and was unable to ignore, desires that totally seduced his logic and better judgment.

He glanced at the clock. He should have been up fifteen minutes ago. He climbed out of bed, quickly showered, and dressed.

Leaving his room, he paused outside Samantha's closed bedroom door. He did not hear any signs of life, nor did he see any light coming from beneath the door. He glanced at his watch. It was five-thirty, past time for her to be up if she intended to help with the barnyard chores. He raised his hand to knock, but caught himself in time. She was a city girl. Even though she'd agreed to help, it was understandable that she would still be sleeping. He suppressed the little pang of disappointment as he continued on to the kitchen.

Halfway across the living room the aroma of fresh coffee hit him, and he realized the kitchen light was on. He paused at the door. A warm smile tugged at the corners of his mouth. Samantha was not only awake, she was dressed and had made coffee. She had also set out the ingredients for breakfast, but seemed hesitant about what to do with them.

"Good morning." He crossed the kitchen to where she stood staring at a large bowl containing a dozen eggs that she had taken from the refrigerator.

She whirled around at the sound of his voice. A little flutter of excitement tingled inside her stomach. He looked so handsome. His silver eyes sparkled with life. His hair was still a little damp from his shower. He was dressed in a wool shirt, jeans and boots, and he looked every bit a cowboy—far removed from trendy. There was something about him that radiated a sensual earthiness—something very appealing and definitely very sexy.

"Good morning to you." She set the bowl of eggs on the counter. "I didn't know what to do about breakfast." She gestured toward the coffeepot. "I hope I made it strong enough this time. I wasn't sure how much coffee to use."

He grabbed a mug from the cupboard. "It smells good." He poured a cup, took a sip, then took a larger swallow. "Tastes great. Hits the spot on a cold snowy morning."

Samantha had not realized she was holding her breath until she suddenly expelled it. She had been anxiously awaiting his response. Once again she was seeking his approval, but she was not sure why. And in a few days at the most—probably sooner, depending on the weather—she would be leaving and they would go their separate ways.

After last night's dinner fiasco Jace automatically took charge of the kitchen. He picked up some eggs from the bowl, then paused for a moment. "What about breakfast? Do you know how to fix eggs?"

Her first reaction was to become defensive about his questions, but she subdued the impulse. It was a legitimate question on his part. "I can do scrambled eggs, but nothing tricky like poached eggs."

He offered her an encouraging smile along with the bowl of eggs. "You tackle these and I'll get the bacon."

Before she was really ready, they had finished eating and it was time to venture outside to take care of the barnyard chores. She pulled on the warm coat, wool cap and gloves he had provided and stood by the front door, waiting for him, her anxiety at full tilt as the oh-so-familiar shudder spread quickly through her body.

Jace pulled on his work gloves, then grabbed his hat from the rack by the front door. He looked at Samantha and offered an encouraging smile. "Are you ready to face the cold, the snow and the chickens?"

She tried to return his smile while projecting an air of confidence, but it felt as if something foreign had been pasted on her face. "Yes, I am. Lead on."

He opened the front door and they stepped out onto the porch in the light of early morning. The icy wind slapped across her face with a shocking sting. She pulled the wool knit cap down over her ears and forehead and covered her nose and cheeks with her gloved hands. Jace had not even paused in his stride. She hurried to catch up with him as he made his way through the snow directly toward the barn. He pulled open the door and they both hurried inside.

Samantha hugged her shoulders and stomped her feet against the ground to shake the snow from her boots. "I've never been this cold in my entire life. I've seen things on the Weather Channel about storms like this one, heard them talking about windchill factors way below zero, but I never imagined how cold that really was...until now." She glanced over at Jace. "How can people live in weather like this?"

Jace was unable to keep the edge of irritation out of his voice. "Some of us find cold and snow invigorating. We enjoy the change of seasons. But I guess you soft city folk wouldn't know about the hearty outdoors and clean air." He pointedly stared at her.

"*Soft city folk!* I'll have you know that I belong to a health club and exercise regularly. Los Angeles is surrounded by mountains and it's only a two-hour drive to Big Bear, where I often go snow skiing in winter. I also cross-country ski. *Normal* cold weather doesn't bother me, and I find my occasional trips to the slopes to be an enjoyable change of pace. But this..." She waved her arm in a broad sweeping gesture toward the barn door. "There's nothing *normal* about what's going on out there." Suddenly she did not feel as cold as she had only moments earlier. He had her blood rushing again, almost the same way as when he kissed her.

Jace looked at her calmly. With her hands on her hips, fire burning in the depths of her eyes, Samantha was the picture of a strong, determined woman, an interesting contrast to the woman who had displayed such a hopeless incompetence in the kitchen. He did not dare say it out loud, the clichéd line that sounded like something from a bad movie, but there was no getting around the fact that she was beautiful when she was angry.

He reached out and brushed the snow from her knit cap and from the shoulders of her coat. He said softly, "Why don't we continue this conversation later? Right now there are chores that need to be done."

Without waiting for any response from her, he headed for the henhouse. She followed close on his heels, running to keep up with his long-legged stride and to stay close enough to hear what he was saying.

"This is a cattle ranch. Our business is not poultry farming. We do keep enough chickens to service our own needs for eggs and meat. During the summer they have an open yard area enclosed with chicken wire where they are free to be inside or outside. During freezing weather they're kept inside under environmental and climate control, proper heat and fresh air circulation. Not only do they have to be fed and watered, but the cages need to be regularly cleaned to avoid disease due to the confined conditions."

He came to an abrupt halt and turned back toward her. She almost ran into him. "This is where the feed is stored. It's a simple process. Fill the bucket." He demonstrated for her, then set the bucket on a bench. "First thing, though, is to make sure they have fresh water." He went into the henhouse. She followed but stopped just inside the door.

Samantha watched as he shooed the unruly birds out of his way, then checked and filled the water containers. She had never been this close to a chicken before—at least not a live one. They looked mean to her, the way they kept ruffling their feathers, and they had beady little eyes. She backed away, edging nearer the door. She may have kept an eye on what Jace was doing, but the majority of her attention was directed toward the chickens. She swallowed hard and tried to appear calm and in control, a far cry from the way her insides felt.

Jace continued with his instructions. "After the water, then you bring in the feed. Part of it goes here." He indicated a trough on the ground. "The rest of it can be scattered around. While the chickens are eating, you can gather the eggs from the nests. You just reach in, take the egg and place it in a basket."

She continued to keep a wary eye on the menacing chickens. "Uh...what if the chicken is sitting on the nest?"

"Then you just reach in under her and take the egg. Not every nest will have an egg, but you need to check them all. Take whatever you find. It's very simple."

"Yes...well, it...uh—" she cleared her throat "—sounds easy. When do I start?"

He cocked his head, a perplexed expression covering his face as if he were surprised by her question. "You start right now. Grab that bucket of feed I left on the bench. You'll find the egg basket next to the feed bin. When you get the eggs back to the kitchen, wash them off and place them in the bowl in the refrigerator."

Jace started to leave, then paused as he drew up beside her. "Are you clear with everything? Do you have any questions?"

"I'm fine. You go ahead with your work. I'll see you later." She shot a surreptitious glance toward the chickens, then watched as Jace exited the henhouse. One of the chickens, a particularly mean-looking hen, flapped its wings and took a couple of steps toward her. She let out a little yelp and made a hasty retreat out the door.

She leaned back against the wall in the safety of the barn, took a deep breath and tried to calm what she knew were irrational fears.

A little shiver darted up her back. She took another steadying breath, then forced herself to retrieve the feed bucket. She turned back toward the henhouse, paused at the door, then quickly opened it and stepped inside.

She halted in midstride and her eyes widened in shock. Where had all the chickens come from? When she and Jace were inside, it had appeared as if there were only about ten or so chickens. Now all of a sudden she was surrounded by what seemed like dozens of vicious birds, flapping their wings and clucking as they ran toward her. She knew, intellectually, that all they wanted was the food she carried in the bucket, but emotionally was a different story.

Samantha tried to muffle her frightened scream and continue with her job. She tried, but she couldn't make any headway. Finally she threw her hands up in the air, sending the feed bucket sailing across the room. She whirled around and ran out the door, almost tripping on a loose plank before she could get to safety. Her chest heaved as she attempted to regain her wits. She peeked back inside the henhouse. The chickens were gobbling up the grain that had been scattered everywhere, totally unconcerned about the person responsible for dropping it.

She stared at the basket, the one to be used for collecting eggs. Now would be the right time, while the chickens were busy eating. She could sneak behind them, check the nests, collect the eggs and then get out. She would have done the required chore. And the next day the storm would be over, and Jace could take her back to her car and she could return to civilization. She could resume her life.

She grabbed the basket and headed back toward the henhouse. She prided herself on always finishing what she started, and she was not about to have this be the first time she left a job undone. There was another reason, too—a reason perhaps even more compelling than her pride. She couldn't bear the thought that Jace might think less of her, that he might think she was a quitter. She didn't seem to be able to get past the need to have his approval. So with a determined breath, she pushed open the door to the henhouse.

Jace had just finished a brief meeting with Ben Downey at the bunkhouse, and reached for his heavy jacket. "Sounds like you have everything under control, Ben. We've had almost a foot of snow since yesterday afternoon, but right now the wind seems to be our major problem. As long as the power lines don't snap, we should be okay."

"I've talked to Sam over at the Double Bar K about sharing the feed drop for the north pastures," Ben told him, dumping the old coffee grounds. "Since we did it last time, he said they'd handle that for us." He put in fresh coffee to make a new pot. "How's your houseguest doing? I swear, I've never seen anyone so ill prepared to be at a ranch."

Jace paused for a moment before answering. It had been an innocent enough question, but it touched a place inside him. "I got her some clothes—"

Ben whirled around, a broad smile covering his face. "Not some of Mom's—why, you could fit two of her inside Mom's clothes."

"No...not Helen's clothes. I...uh...gave her some of Stephanie's clothes that I had packed away. They seem to fit her okay." He paused for a moment, a little wave of uncertainty washing over his thoughts.

Ben placed his hand on Jace's shoulder for a brief moment in a gesture of comfort.

"Anyway..." Jace returned his thoughts to the business at hand. "I've left her with the chickens. She's going to feed them, then collect the eggs."

"Well, that little city gal didn't look to me like she was gonna be much of a hand around a ranch."

Jace chuckled softly. "I can tell you that she's certainly no help around the kitchen. Hopefully she'll do better with the barnyard chores." He glanced at his watch as he pulled on his jacket. "I think I'll check on her before heading to the stables."

He put on his gloves and hat as he looked out the window at the blowing snow. The howling sound of the wind had been steady all morning without letup. He opened the door and dashed across the open ground, headed toward the barn, bucking a strong head wind all the way.

The feed bucket was not by the bin, and the egg basket was also missing. He opened the door to the hen-house and almost burst out laughing. The bucket was on its side on the ground with feed scattered everywhere. And Samantha...the look of terror that covered her face was a picture truly worth a thousand words. She had such a tight grip on the handle of the egg basket that her knuckles had almost turned white. Every time one of the hens looked her way she flinched. When one of them actually took a couple of steps in her direction she physically jumped aside and squealed.

He watched her a moment longer. She tentatively reached into an empty nest, withdrew an egg and placed it in the basket with the three other eggs she had already gathered. She moved down the line to the next one and stared at the hen sitting on the nest. The hen stared back at her. She hesitated, then passed it by.

A flutter of noise caught her attention. She looked down and saw two hens rushing toward her, flapping their wings and emitting angry sounds. The chickens were attacking her! It was too much for her. She turned and ran blindly toward the door. This time she was not as lucky with the loose floor plank. She tripped and went sprawling flat on her face. The basket hit the ground, and the few eggs she had managed to collect smashed into a gooey mess.

She started to scramble to her feet when her gaze lit on the last thing she wanted to see. There, right in front of her face, was a pair of boots. She reluctantly looked up and found Jace staring down at her, amusement twinkling in his silver eyes. She felt the heated flush of embarrassment creep across her face and neck. She opened her mouth to speak, but no words came out.

His face held an expression of feigned innocence. "Is there a problem here?" He reached out and helped her to her feet. "Where were you headed in such a hurry?"

His voice teased her, at least she hoped that was what he was doing, rather than criticizing her behavior—or worse yet, showing his contempt. She felt bad enough on her own. Once she was on her feet, he didn't release her, and she allowed him to continue to hold her. It felt so good in his arms. It was warm and safe yet produced a tingling thread of excitement that expanded until it filled her senses.

When she didn't answer him, his amusement turned to concern and he released her from his embrace. "Are you all right?" He pulled off his gloves, then reached out and brushed the dirt from the side of her face. "Did you hurt yourself?'' His fingertips lingered against her cheek.

"No...I..." She brushed at the dirt from the front of her coat and jeans. "I think I'm okay."

She stared down at the broken eggs, afraid to make eye contact with him. She felt the anger welling inside her, anger directed toward herself. He had rescued her from a potentially dangerous situation, and all he'd asked in return was her help with a few simple chores.

She finally forced herself to look at his face, to look into his eyes. Her voice quavered as she spoke. "I'm so very sorry. I seem to have made a real mess of things."

The obvious depth of her concern surprised him. "Hey, it's not that bad. Don't worry about it."

"But look what I've done. I broke all the eggs."

He chuckled softly. "You didn't collect all that many." He stared at the broken eggs for a moment. "I only see four broken eggs. There's probably a dozen more...at least." He picked up the egg basket from the ground. "Come on, I'll give you a hand."

She looked as if she were going to burst out in tears any second. The vulnerability she tried so hard to hide reached out and touched him. "Things aren't that bad." He turned up the sides of her mouth with his fingers until a shy smile appeared. He offered her an encouraging smile of his own. "There...that's much better. Let's go collect some eggs."

He took her hand and led her back into the henhouse. She managed to stay behind him rather than next to him. "Now, the first rule of egg collecting is to make sure the chickens know exactly who is in charge."

"I think that was the problem." She laughed nervously, trying to cover the level of her anxiety. "It was the chickens who were in charge, and they made sure I knew it.''

"I guess I'll just have to teach you a few tricks about dealing with chickens so that won't happen again.'' He turned to face her, still clutching her hand. ''Are you game?'' He gave her hand a squeeze.

She had expected him to admonish her for the broken eggs and the chaos she had created from a simple task. Instead he had been understanding and forgiving. She returned the squeeze. ''Sure.''

She watched as he demonstrated the fine art of egg gathering, then stayed with her as she tried her hand at it. He had been correct. It was easy. When she finished, she proudly displayed the basket containing sixteen eggs. There would have been twenty in all. ''Now I take the eggs to the kitchen, wash them and put them in the large bowl in the refrigerator?''

"That's it.'' He opened the henhouse door and stepped aside so she could go ahead of him.

They returned to the ranch house where Samantha quickly finished without further incident. She put on her warm jacket, knit cap and gloves, then picked up the egg basket. ''I'll return this to the barn, then be right back.''

Jace watched from the window as she hurried across the yard. Then he turned his attention to the weather. There seemed to be a lull in the unrelenting wind, and the heavy snowfall had momentarily let up. A thought popped into his mind. With a mischievous grin, he pulled on his warm jacket and headed for the front door.

Samantha exited the barn, being careful to close the door tightly. Even though the storm seemed to have calmed down, she hurried across the yard toward the warmth of the house. Then it happened. She was out in the open, unprotected, an easy target. The soft mushy snow splattered against her shoulder.

"Hey! What the—" She whirled around and saw Jace holding another snowball. A playful grin spread across his handsome face. She quickly sized up the situation and instinctively retaliated. She scooped a handful of snow, packed it into a round ball and threw it in his direction. It had been a long time since she'd participated in such a carefree moment of fun.

Jace laughed as he ducked the snowball hurtling through the air with deadly accuracy. "That's some snowball pitching arm you have. You weren't kidding when you said you spent time in the mountains in winter."

"That was a very smooth maneuver you just made, too. You've got quick reflexes. Next time, however, you won't be so lucky." She laughed as she scooped up another handful of snow and quickly packed it into a ball. It felt good to laugh. Just then, a hint of sadness touched her reality. Laughing was something she did not do very often anymore, something she did not seem to have time for. It was a situation she should correct...but how?

"No you don't. Baseball may be your game, but..." Before she realized what he was up to, he rushed toward her. "Football's my game." He tackled her around the waist, dragging her down to the snow with him.

She screamed and laughed at the same time, struggling to escape his hold. "Not fair!"

"*Not fair* you say?" He grinned mischievously at her as he grabbed a handful of snow.

Her eyes widened as she realized what he planned to do. She struggled in his arms while trying to push him away. "No...please...you wouldn't dare—" Her laughter cut off her words.

"Oh, yes. I most certainly would dare." He quickly squished the soft snow in her face—the soft, wet, cold snow. "Take that, Miss Burkett. Now, do you give up, or am I going to have to teach you another lesson?"

She stopped struggling, a calculated move on her part to gain the upper hand—lull him into the sense that he had won the battle. As soon as she felt him loosen his grip on her she swiftly wiggled out of his grasp, grabbed a handful of snow and stuffed it down the back of his shirt. "Me give up? Never!"

"Aaargh! That's cold!" He tried to catch hold of her but she scrambled to her feet, deftly avoiding his attempt to grab her. "You come back here!" He jumped to his feet, yanked out his shirttail, and reached up his back to brush away the snow. He turned toward her. She stood with a snowball in her hand, taunting him with her grin—daring him to try and come after her.

His sly grin and the twinkle in his eyes spoke louder than his words. "Now you've done it—this is war!"

She let loose with the snowball, striking him against the chest, then immediately scooped up another handful of snow and threw it at him. Before she could strike a third time, however, he attacked her with a barrage of snowballs. Three...four...five...he did not give her time to retaliate. She put her arms in front of her head to protect herself from the cold, wet assault.

"Do you give up yet?" His words chided, yet his voice was filled with fun.

She looked up just in time to have a wet glob of snow glance against her cheek. "Never!" She quickly scooped another handful of snow and packed it into a round ball...but not quickly enough.

He moved swiftly, pinning her to the ground. She felt his body press down on top of her. He held her wrists together in the strong grip of one hand as he shoveled a mound of snow with his other hand. She struggled as best she could, shaking her head from side to side, all the while laughing. She kicked out, trying to dislodge him. He quickly moved his leg across hers, severely limiting her movements.

"How about now?" He dribbled some of the snow onto her forehead then touched some of it to the tip of her nose. "Are you ready to say uncle?"

"I give...I give..." Her own giggles momentarily cut off her words. "Uncle. Great-uncle! Everyone's uncle!" She saw his smile fade as his gaze locked with hers in an intense moment.

His face was very close to hers, and slowly he released her wrists from his grip. He felt his heart beat a little faster; his breath came a little quicker. He became aware of just how much of her body was beneath him. He moved his leg from across hers. His voice conveyed a slight huskiness that surprised him when he heard it. "I—I'd better get back to work." He searched the depths of her eyes. "There's still lots to do."

With his body pressing hers into the soft snow and their faces almost touching, her insides began to tremble. Once again, the feeling had nothing to do with the weather. The snow may have been cold, but there was no mistaking the heated desire burning within her.

She brushed the snow from his hair before allowing her gloved hand to come to rest against his cheek. Her voice contained just a hint of uncertainty. "Yes...I'm sure you have lots of work to do."

He seemed to search the depths of her eyes for a moment longer, then lowered his head and captured her mouth. His kiss started out soft, but quickly escalated.

She felt the demand of his too-long-pent-up passions, felt the excitement he stirred within her. She again responded to his kiss, allowing it to continue for several seconds before breaking off. There was no mistaking the ardor that existed between them. There was no mistaking the hunger and desire conveyed by his kiss. She held his steady, unwavering gaze for a moment longer.

"Jace...I'm not sure this is such a good idea." Those were her words, but they certainly were not her thoughts and feelings. It had been a long time since she had allowed herself to break loose and act like a kid. She had almost forgotten what fun just for the sake of fun was all about.

"What's not a good idea? The snowball fight?" He brushed his lips against hers again. A sensual warmth enveloped his words. "Or the kiss?" He captured her mouth without giving her an opportunity to answer.

The heat they generated nearly melted the snow around them. The depth of feeling quickly escalated. He slipped his tongue between her lips and brushed it against the texture of hers. It was a moment that affected each of them very deeply. They lay in the snow, wrapped in each other's arms. There was no way this could be ignored, no way they could pretend it had not happened.

"Hey, Jace..." The voice came from the bunkhouse, followed by the appearance of Ben Downey. "Just got the latest weather forecast. It don't look—" He came to an abrupt halt when he spotted Jace and Samantha in each other's arms and almost buried in the snow.

Ben's voice carried all the embarrassment that also

covered his face. "Oops. Sorry. I didn't mean to... uh..." He turned back toward the bunkhouse.

"Hold on, Ben." Jace quickly rose to his feet and held out his hand to help Samantha.

Ben stared at the ground, then back toward the barn. "I didn't mean to interrupt—"

"You didn't interrupt anything, Ben. We were..." Jace shot a helpless glance toward Samantha. He was seldom caught off guard or at a loss for words, but this was one of those times.

"We were engaged in a snowball fight." She addressed her comments to Ben as she stepped in to fill the awkward lull in the conversation. "I think your boss discovered, much to his surprise, that he'd met his match." She couldn't totally hide an amused grin.

The same amused grin tugged at the corners of Jace's mouth. "I do have to admit that she's got a wicked throwing arm." A soft warmth spread through his body as he also recalled the passion of their kiss.

Jace moved quickly to bring things back into an impersonal mode. "What's the latest on this weather?" Even as he asked, he could feel the wind pick up.

"The full force of this storm should hit sometime late tomorrow. They're saying we could get well over three feet of snow out of this over the next few days. Bad winds gusting to near gale force and cold temperatures. This part of the state will be brought to a virtual standstill—roads closed, airports shut down."

"Have we got everything under control? Anything left to do?" Jace asked.

"We're covered. Vince has the power generator on standby and the three snowmobiles and the Sno-Cat are all tuned and ready. We'll be able to get to the outlying pastures if absolutely necessary."

Jace looked at the angry sky and heaved a sigh, more of concern than relief. "Well, I guess there's nothing left to do but ride it out." He returned his attention to Ben. "You let me know about any changes, even if it's under control."

"Sure thing, Jace." Ben touched the brim of his hat and nodded toward Samantha, a hint of embarrassment again darting across his face. "Ma'am." He turned and hurried back toward the bunkhouse.

Jace put his arm around Samantha's shoulder. The casual gesture seemed natural, not at all awkward or out of place. It felt comfortable. It felt very right. They returned to the ranch house, neither saying anything as they walked along together.

They each knew that this time they could not ignore what had happened by simply pretending it never occurred. The kiss had been filled with more than simply heated passions. It had conveyed a hint of things yet to be, an anticipation of a sensual togetherness that promised to be beyond what either of them had imagined.

Five

Dinner was over and the dishes were done. Jace and Samantha sat on the floor in front of the fireplace, the light from the burning logs providing the only illumination in the room. The golden glow settled across their faces. Music played quietly in the background. The air literally crackled with the sexual energy that sizzled between them.

He drew her to him until she was seated between his legs with her back resting against his chest. He draped his arms casually around her shoulders and grasped one of her hands between his two. Her other hand lay alongside his outer thigh, and she nestled her head back against his shoulder.

His words tickled softly across her ear. ''Tell me about yourself. I know you're from Los Angeles and work as an efficiency expert, but that's about it. You never did say exactly what brought you to this area. You flew to Denver to visit a friend and somehow ended up in Wyoming.''

"It's a long story. A stupid tale that wouldn't be very interesting.'' His question had brought mixed feelings. On one hand she wanted to put the bad experience behind her and not think about it. But a stronger force said she wanted to be open with him, to share something personal.

His voice contained a sincere level of deep caring. "I'd like to hear about it…if you're willing to share.''

She was willing to share, but she was not too sure Jerry Kensington should be the subject of that sharing. She swallowed down the trepidation and plunged ahead.

"I like everything in my life to be carefully planned and organized. I'm not comfortable with uncontrolled situations. People say I'm compulsive about things.'' She paused for a moment before continuing. "I guess they're right. My fiancé—''

"*Fiancé?*" Jace's muscles tensed, and a quick intake of breath filled his lungs. He jerked upright as he released her hand. Several feelings instantly coursed through him—anger, hurt and finally confusion. "You…you're engaged to be married? I thought—''

"No!'' She twisted around to face him. She saw it in his eyes, the myriad of emotions. "I *was* engaged…'' She allowed her gaze to dart away for a moment, then return to his eyes. "I'm not engaged anymore. That's all part of what I'm doing here, why I went to Denver.''

She closed her eyes for an instant to collect her thoughts and formulate her words. A warm sensation flowed through her as he enveloped her in his embrace again and pulled her body close to his.

The comfortable familiarity of his arms calmed her anxiety. "My ex-fiancé lives in Denver. He was always giving me a hard time about never doing anything on the spur of the moment, of always having to plan out my every move. I decided to surprise him with an unannounced visit.'' She shifted her weight into a more comfortable position, making sure she did not dislodge his embrace. ''Well, I surprised him all right. He was in bed with another woman.''

He tightened his hold on her, as much an offer of comfort as a desire to hold her closer. ''I'm sorry. That must have been very awkward, very uncomfortable... and very painful.''

''Awkward...definitely. Uncomfortable...not as much as you would think. Painful?'' She was silent for a moment as the memories flooded over her. ''It was very painful, but now that I've had time to think about it I'm not sure exactly what was hurt—my emotions or my pride.''

She exhibited such a refreshing candor, not at all what he had expected. With each passing minute she had managed to work her way farther and farther under his skin. While his physical desire for her continued to run rampant through his body, his feelings seemed to be reaching out on a more personal level.

''Do you think...'' He was not sure he really wanted to ask his next question. More important, he was not sure he wanted to know the answer. ''Do you think there's any chance of the two of you working this out and getting back together? If you've invested a lot of time in a relationship, then maybe you shouldn't let it go so quickly.''

She thought about what he'd said. It was the same thing she'd said to herself, the same thing she'd argued about with herself. It was not a matter of whether it could be saved. The reality was that she didn't want to save it. The whole thing had been bad from the beginning, and now she knew it for sure.

"You're not saying anything I haven't already given a lot of thought. The truth is, there just wasn't that much invested. There was time, but it hadn't been quality time. I'd been harboring sincere doubts for quite a while. The main reason I decided to make the trip was to elicit some sort of reassurance that the relationship was solid. I think I always knew, deep down, that it was never going to work."

He placed a gentle kiss on her cheek. "I'm sorry."

"In retrospect I think I felt relief more than anything else. Everything was finally out in the open, and we both knew it was over."

"But how...why did you end up here in Wyoming? Why didn't you go back to the airport and take the first plane home?"

"I don't know...I guess I was in such a state of shock and confusion that I just started driving without thinking about where I was going. By the time I realized how stupid I was acting, I was lost. Next I got stuck in that snowdrift when I tried to find my way back to the highway." She turned her head, looked back at him over her shoulder and offered a shy and somewhat embarrassed smile. "And the rest you know." She expelled a sigh. "Pretty pathetic, wouldn't you say?"

"No, I wouldn't say that." He leaned forward, nuzzled the side of her neck, then kissed her on the cheek. "What I would say is that you were fortunate to find out before you married him. I know that's a pretty clichéd response, but I think it's true. Besides, this guy obviously didn't appreciate what he had, and it's my opinion that you're better off without him."

"Well, you seem to have an opinion on just about

everything." The words were said without inflection, without any hidden meaning. They were stated as a simple fact.

Jace did not take exception to what she had said. "I have lots of opinions, some I hold more dearly than others."

They sat quietly for several minutes enjoying the music and the warmth of the fire. An unusual sensation settled over Samantha, a lightness of spirit, as if merely talking about it had put the matter to rest once and for all. The shock and stab of pain the confrontation with Jerry Kensington had caused had now been reduced to nothing more than an unpleasant part of her past. That in itself confirmed her suspicions that she really had not loved Jerry.

Her thoughts turned to Jace's house, to the generations of the Tremayne family who had lived in the warmth of these surroundings. They were happy times. She could feel the love that had existed in the house. Did that apply to Jace, too? Did she dare ask?

She didn't turn to look at him, preferring to ask her question without being able to see the reaction on his face. "I was wondering about these clothes. You said they belonged to your wife." She hesitated for a moment, not sure of how to proceed. "Your wife...she doesn't live here anymore? You're...uh...divorced?" She became instantly aware of the tremor that darted through his body. She was glad she couldn't see his face, and sorry she'd asked the question.

"I guess I should have said something about it earlier. It's just...well, I haven't really talked about it for a long time." He tightened his hold on her and took a calming breath. "Stephanie...my wife...died in an automobile accident. It was four years ago." Then he added, with a hint of poignancy surrounding his words, "She was pregnant with our first child."

His words stunned her. She immediately turned around so she could see him. It was not at all what she had expected to hear. She saw the pain in his eyes, but it seemed to belong to the past rather than a current grieving process. "I'm so sorry, I shouldn't have asked. I didn't mean to pry."

"It's all right." He brushed her hair away from her cheek as he searched her face and finally settled on her eyes. "I came to terms with it long ago." He might have exaggerated the amount of time that had passed since that acceptance, but it was true. He'd finally come to terms with the tragedy, but it wasn't until he'd opened the trunk that he'd begun to feel a sense of closure.

A new closeness existed between them, one born from the trust required to expose emotional scars. Something else existed, too. There was a longing, an unanswered hunger gnawing at each of them...a hunger that seemed to have only one answer, only one solution.

Jace leaned back against the floor pillows, drawing her body tightly against his. They had the entire night ahead of them, a night filled with many possibilities. He lowered his head and took complete possession of her mouth. His actions clearly stated what he wanted, without imposing a demanding control.

Samantha had absolutely no objections to his unspoken intentions. She was not a promiscuous woman. It was not like her to be so accommodating after knowing a man such a short period of time, but Jace Tremayne fired up her desires in a way Jerry Kensington never had. She didn't understand it and she couldn't explain it, but she knew it was useless to deny these feelings. She wrapped her arms around his neck and lost herself in the heat of his passion.

There was no hesitation this time. Jace twined his tongue with hers and was surprised by a fiery response that almost knocked him for a loop—not what he'd expected from this compulsively organized woman who had to have everything planned out in advance.

It had been four years since he'd been with a woman, four years since he'd made love. It had also been four years since he had met a woman who aroused any real desire in him. Samantha Burkett was most certainly that woman. Everything about her excited him—the smoothness of her skin, the way the silky strands of her hair feathered against her face, the addictive taste of her delectable mouth. He wanted to know more of her. He wanted to intimately know all of her. Slowly, almost without realizing, he pulled her over on top of him.

He savored the dark, moist recess of her mouth as he ran his fingers through her hair, with his hand finally coming to rest cupping the back of her head. His other hand traced along her hip then across the curve of her bottom. Even through the denim of her jeans he could feel the heat of her body radiating to every part of him. His very real arousal pressed hard against the front of his jeans.

He rolled her over on her back, until his body covered hers. He pulled his face away from hers just enough to look into her eyes. They sparkled with life and the promise of an incendiary excitement he could feel all the way to his toes. He ran his fingers through her hair, brushing it back from her face.

"Samantha..." He was not sure exactly what he wanted to say or, more accurately, how to say it. He feared that he would appear clumsy and awkward. "It's

been a long time since...well, since I—'' He again
seized her mouth, unable to complete his sentence.

Samantha wanted to put a stop to what was happening
before it was too late, yet she did not want it to stop.
There was nothing subtle about the way Jace Tremayne
made her feel. She'd been caught up in a whirlwind from
the moment he'd plucked her out of that snowdrift, a
whirlwind that had become more and more dangerous
with each passing hour.

She wasn't sure how much he wanted, how much he
would ask for, how much he would try to take. She was
sure, however, that she was willing to give him whatever
that was. The decision was a momentous one for her, a
spontaneous choice. She knew if she took the time to
analyze and agonize over what was happening, it would
truly frighten her. Any further thoughts evaporated in the
heat of his passion.

Jace wasn't sure how far to take things. He thrust his
tongue into her mouth, twining with hers in a seduction
that left no doubt about where they were headed. His
other moves, however, were more tentative in nature. He
knew what he wanted. For the first time in four years he
had a clear picture of what could be, but he was not sure
exactly what to do. It had been so long since he had
played the game.

The game—a game was certainly not what he wanted
this to be. He did not know how things could have happened so quickly, how his thoughts and feelings had
crystallized so completely in such a short period of time.
What he lacked in confidence, however, he made up for
in desire...genuine, sincere and deeply felt.

He tugged at the bottom of her sweater, then inched
his hand underneath. His fingers tickled up the bare skin
of her rib cage, then grazed the side of her breast. The

sensual flow spread from his fingers up his arm, then throughout his body. His heart pounded against his chest.

Samantha's skin tingled beneath his touch. She felt the hardness of his arousal press against her thigh, a hardness she imagined she could almost feel deep inside her. She threaded her fingers through his thick hair. Her eyes snapped open when his hand closed over the lacy bra cup covering her breast. Reality intruded into the intimacy that existed between them.

Jace felt her body stiffen. He quickly withdrew his hand from beneath her sweater. He saw the look in her eyes. Relief settled over him when he realized it wasn't anger he was seeing. Hesitation or uncertainty perhaps, but not anger.

"Samantha? What's wrong?"

She knew it was a valid question. Exactly what *was* wrong? Nervousness? The jitters? She certainly was not a naive innocent who had never made love before, and just the thought of making love with Jace Tremayne actually scorched her sensibilities right down to her toes. But still... "I think we might be moving too quickly, rushing things a bit. After all, we've only known each other for..." Her voice trailed off. She was sure her words did not sound any more convincing to Jace than they did to her.

He continued to hold her, his body pressing down on top of hers. His voice was soft, soothing. "I know that what you're saying about our knowing each other for such a short amount of time is certainly true. But is there some rule that says you must know someone for a specific period of time before things can move forward? Is the length of time you've known someone more important than what you feel? More important than what you know to be true?"

The mood change was subtle, but they were each keenly aware of it. The attraction between them was no longer about sex, about performance, about living up to assumed expectations. Samantha seemed to be as nervous and uncertain as he was. The clumsiness and awkwardness he feared would ruin the intimacy between them vanished to be replaced by caring. He rolled off her, but continued to hold her close. He nestled her head against his shoulder and caressed her back. His voice became a whisper, perhaps the words for his own benefit rather than hers. "Maybe it is better to slow things down a little."

The storm sent the wind howling around the corners of the house. An occasional strong gust caused the ceiling timbers to creak. The logs in the fireplace popped and crackled, and the flames danced. But Jace and Samantha were barely aware of any of it. They leaned back against the large pillows, enjoying an evening of relaxed closeness. They talked for hours—close, personal, relaxed conversation—yet the time seemed to pass so quickly.

Samantha rested her head on Jace's shoulder as he stroked her hair. "I think the thing that disturbs me the most about being stranded at your ranch—"

Jace felt an uneasiness start in the pit of his stomach and quickly rise. Somewhere in the back of his mind he had hoped she would want to stay for a while. She had already said she had two weeks off from her job and didn't have any other plans—other than her original plan of visiting her then fiancé. He returned his attention to what she was saying.

"Is not having my suitcase." She turned and looked

at him, as if a sudden realization had struck her. "I didn't mean to sound ungrateful, and I certainly appreciate your lending me these clothes. I just meant that it would be nice if I had my own things."

"I'm sure it would be more comfortable for you. Unfortunately—" He cocked his head and listened as the wind whistled at the windows.

She smiled. "I know. It wasn't a very practical thought. Just wishful thinking, that's all." She snuggled her body against his again. He put his arms around her, enclosing her in the warmth of his embrace. For the first time in her life she felt truly at peace.

Jace hurried across the yard toward the bunkhouse. Every few feet he would glance up at the sky, not that he could really see much in the predawn light other than what the security lights picked up. He tried to convince himself that the storm had calmed down, that the wind was not blowing as hard and the snowfall was not as heavy.

Ben Downey looked up as the intrusion of cold air whipped in the door when Jace entered. He held up the coffeepot and an empty mug. "Want some?"

Jace stomped the snow from his boots. "Sure do!"

Ben handed him the mug of hot coffee. "What brings you out here?" Concern darted across his face. "Is something wrong?"

"No." He took a sip of the coffee. "Nothing like that. I just wanted to get your opinion." He jerked his head toward the door. "Have you been outside yet?"

"Yeah, I've already taken a quick tour and everything seems okay. Why?"

"What do you think…would Vince be able to make

a run out across the back pasture in the Sno-Cat without any trouble?"

Ben looked at him quizzically for a moment. "Out across the back pasture? What on earth for?"

"Well..." Jace glanced down at the floor. He could feel his embarrassment spreading across his face. "I...thought maybe we could get to Samantha's car... get her suitcase for her." He looked up again. "What do you think?"

Ben set down his coffee cup. His voice was very matter-of-fact, his expression not registering whatever he might have been thinking. "I'll find Vince and put it to him. I think it needs to be his call."

"Of course. I don't want him trying it if he feels it's too risky."

They found Vince in the bunkhouse kitchen. Ben started to speak, but Jace quickly took control of the conversation. It was his personal favor they were discussing, so he needed to make the request personally rather than leaving the task to his foreman.

Vince pondered the request for a moment. "Well...I'll tell ya, Jace. I don't see as we're talkin' life 'n' death here. If it was somethin' to do with the livestock, then I'd sure give it a try. But since it ain't, I'd rather wait till things calm down a bit."

"I'll leave it up to you, Vince. Whenever you think it's safe. I don't want you taking any unnecessary chances. Like you said, it's not a life-or-death matter."

When Samantha awoke, one of her first thoughts was about making another foray into the henhouse. She was determined to get the job done without any help from Jace and hoped she would be able to finish before she ran into him. It was more than just wanting to prove to

Jace that she could do it. She'd always been self-reliant.
She needed to prove to herself that she could conquer
this situation, too.

The chickens weren't the only thing on her mind. The
previous night's intimacies and the knowledge of where
the evening could easily have led concerned her. She
was afraid that the cold light of dawn might make the
atmosphere between them awkward and strained. She
hoped not, but was unsure.

When she got to the kitchen, Jace had already made
coffee but didn't seem to be in the house. She quickly
downed a glass of orange juice, then put on the warm
jacket, cap and gloves, and stepped out onto the front
porch. She hurried across the yard, focused solely on the
chores that needed to be done.

She filled the feed bucket, then paused at the door of
the henhouse. Taking a steadying breath, she opened the
door and quickly stepped inside. The feeding went almost without incident. She nervously jumped aside a
couple of times, but managed to get the chickens properly fed. But the egg gathering was once again pretty
much a disaster. She managed to collect only six eggs
while breaking almost as many and leaving at least a
dozen in the nests guarded by hostile chickens intent on
doing her harm.

She took her meager results to the kitchen, washed
them and added them to the large bowl in the refrigerator. There had to be an easier way to accomplish things,
and she was sure she could come up with it if she put
her mind and her organizational skills to the matter. After all, that was what she did for a living. She evaluated
work procedures, then found a more efficient way of
achieving the same result. She went to the den to make
herself comfortable while studying the problem.

Jace had breakfast at the bunkhouse with the ranch hands, then embarked on a busy morning work schedule. It was nearly lunchtime when he returned to the house. He refused to accept the notion that he was purposely avoiding Samantha, but he feared she might be harboring feelings of regret over the previous night's closeness. He hoped that was not the case. He'd relished that closeness. He savored each and every moment they'd shared. And he wanted much more.

He paused at the door of the den and watched her for a moment, her brow furrowed in concentration as she studied the paper she held. She seemed very intent on something. He stepped inside the room.

"What are you so serious about?" He detected the nervousness in his voice. Hopefully she would not.

Samantha looked up when his voice intruded into her thoughts. "Jace...I didn't hear you come in." She rose from her chair. "Have you had a busy morning? How's the storm doing? It's been about three hours since I returned from the henhouse. Any letup on the horizon?" Inane, stupid questions—all of them. She was pushing too hard. She needed to calm down. She took a couple of deep breaths.

"You look as if something's bothering you." He offered an encouraging smile as he crossed the room toward her. "Anything I can help with?" he asked as he reached her side. Every feeling he had experienced the night before came back full force. He searched her face then settled on her eyes. A moment later his mouth covered hers.

His kiss was now familiar to her, yet it held every bit as much excitement as the very first time his lips had brushed against hers. The awkwardness she had feared vanished the second they came into physical contact. He put his arms around her waist and pulled her to him as she slipped her arms around his neck. It was a long, lingering kiss filled with both soft sensuality and heated fervor. But of much more importance was the fact that it felt so natural, as if they had been together for years...as if they belonged together.

Jace finally pulled back from Samantha, pausing long enough to place a quick kiss on her forehead. "How did you make out with the chickens?"

"Well...the feeding went okay, but I still had a little problem with the eggs. I'm afraid I broke some of them again..." Embarrassment crept into her voice. "And there were others that I couldn't get to."

"Couldn't get to? What do you mean?" There were two particularly troublesome hens who occasionally attempted to lay their eggs in strange, out-of-the-way places. He allowed a slight scowl to cross his face. He hoped they had not reverted to their old ways.

She took a quick step back. A flash of irritation ignited inside her. "I meant just what I said. I wasn't able to collect them. When I reached into the nests the chickens tried to bite—" She cut off her words as soon as she saw his expression. Was she reading more into it than was there, or was she seeing his displeasure at her clumsiness?

She took a calming breath. Now was the opportune time to present her idea. "I've been giving the problem quite a bit of thought this morning, and I think I've come up with an idea that will make the feeding and egg collecting more efficient. I've made a sketch—"

He took an involuntary step backward as his eyes widened in genuine surprise. "Excuse me? Did I hear you correctly?" He could not stop the tickle that threatened to turn into an amused chuckle. "You have some sort of plan that will improve the task of feeding a few chickens and gathering some eggs?''

His attitude—what she perceived as a verbal attack—caught her completely off guard. She jumped to defend her position. "This is what I do for a living—analyze work procedures and make them more efficient by streamlining the operation.''

The incredulity of it all smacked him in the face. He blurted out his immediate reaction without thinking. ''You've got to be kidding!''

Six

She couldn't have been more shocked if he'd physically slapped her across the face. She opened her mouth, but no words came out.

He continued, oblivious to the adverse effect his words had caused. "I think I'd be safe in saying that your experience with chickens, either feeding or egg gathering, is very limited at best."

Her irritation flared into anger. "I'll have you know that I've studied a wide variety of production techniques and facilities—factory assembly lines, mass market publications, nationwide food distribution systems, and even housing construction. I think—"

The amused chuckle he had been trying to suppress finally turned into genuine laughter. "Whoa, hold on there. I know I said this before, but apparently I didn't make myself very clear. This is *not* a poultry farm. We do not raise chickens for market nor do we sell eggs.

The primary business of this ranch is beef cattle. We also have a couple of dairy cows, but that doesn't mean that we're in the milk business. Beef cattle...that's what we do here.''

He continued, not allowing her an opportunity to speak. ''I'm sure you're very good at your job, but I think it's only fair to mention that I have a degree in animal husbandry. I subscribe to several journals and attend seminars on a regular basis. I was even invited to be a guest lecturer at the university a couple of years ago, the topic being the running of a successful cattle ranch in today's economic climate. I would think—''

''Uh...sorry to interrupt, but we got a problem.''

Jace whirled around at the sound of Ben Downey's voice. His attention had been so focused on Samantha that he hadn't heard Ben come in. Embarrassment covered Ben's face like a blanket, telling of his obvious discomfiture at having intruded into the disagreement between Jace and Samantha.

''Problem?'' Jace's long-legged stride quickly took him across the den to the hallway where Ben waited.

''Yeah...'' Ben's voice faded off as he and Jace hurried away, leaving a perplexed Samantha standing alone in the middle of the room. A few moments later she heard the front door open and close, then all was quiet except for the ever-present howl of the icy wind.

She slumped into a large easy chair and sat there for several minutes without moving. She felt as if all the air had been knocked from her sails. Emotion fought logic as she carefully and thoroughly digested each and every one of the words he had thrown at her. The result left her somewhat uncertain about what to do.

She stared at the piece of paper still clutched in her hand. She studied the silly little sketch and read the notes

she had jotted down. How pompous they sounded, how
very pretentious. By her own admission she had never
been on a farm or a ranch in her entire life. She crumpled
the sheet of paper into a ball and tossed it in the waste
basket. He was right. She had no business offering suggestions when she couldn't perform the simplest of barnyard tasks without making a mess of it.

She rose to her feet, took a deep breath and slowly
expelled it, then clenched her jaw in determination. One
way or the other she would show him that she was not
the incompetent woman he obviously took her to be.
This had nothing to do with the tremors of excitement
his touch caused, or the way his kisses lit a fire inside
her, hotter than anything she had ever known.

This was a matter of pride, pure and simple. She could
not have someone as dynamic as Jace Tremayne thinking she was a helpless ninny. She would prove to him
just how capable and efficient she really was...and how
adaptable she could be. Of course, being adaptable was
another area where she had almost no experience.

Once again, she reminded herself, Samantha Burkett
sought the approval of someone in her life. In the past
the need had been linked to the approval of her parents—first directly, then through her career accomplish-
ments, and finally through a successful marriage to Jerry
Kensington. None of her efforts had given her the elu-
sive acceptance she so desired.

This time was different. It was important to her—not
for her parents, not for her career, but for her personally.
This time, for the first time, she realized that she didn't
need the approval. This time she *wanted* it, and she
wanted it for herself.

Loosen up, go with the flow. The words had been Jerry
Kensington's, and as much as it displeased her to agree

with anything he said, she knew it was true. That topic of discussion might have been different from the near argument she'd just had with Jace, but the dynamic was exactly the same. Accept things for what they are and stop trying to improve everything. Some things simply do not need to be improved. She felt good about the realization. It was a positive step forward. Maybe not a large one, but a step down the right path just the same.

She spent the rest of the day alone. Whatever the problem was that had so abruptly grabbed Jace's attention, it kept him busy for the entire day. She curled up with a book, choosing the chair by the large window in the living room where she could keep an eye on what was happening outside. Every now and then she would catch a glimpse of Jace or Ben, usually in the company of at least one other man, as they dashed from one building to another.

It was nearly dark when Jace finally returned to the house. It had been a rough day for him. She saw it on his face and in his eyes. He collapsed into what was obviously his favorite chair and didn't move for several minutes. At first she thought he'd fallen asleep, then he slowly opened his eyes and glanced around the room until his gaze fell on her.

She offered a tentative smile. "You look tired."

The weariness was evident in his voice. "I am. A section of the roof on the stables caved in. We had to do emergency repairs. The cold and the snow were bad enough, but add that bitter wind and it was the most miserable day I've had in a long time."

"Is everything okay? Are the horses all right?"

"Yeah, they're fine. Fortunately they were in the other end of the building." He forced himself to sit upright, paused a moment, then pulled off his boots and dropped them on the floor with a loud thud.

"Can I get you anything?" She picked up his boots and carried them to the front door, placing them next to the boots she had worn that morning. "Maybe something to eat?"

"Later, but right now I think I'd like a scotch and water if you'd be good enough to pour." He arched an eyebrow and cocked his head. "Would you join me?"

"Well…"

He held out his hand toward her and flashed an inviting smile. "A peace offering?" He had spent a good part of the afternoon mentally kicking himself for making an issue of her attempts to reorganize the henhouse.

She returned his smile. "Yes, I'd like that."

He watched as she went to the liquor cabinet and took down the bottle of scotch and two glasses. He didn't really have any quarrel with what he'd said to her. He still believed he was right. She had no business trying to tell him how to run his ranch especially when she had already admitted to having absolutely no expertise in the matter. His unhappiness stemmed from the way he'd handled it. She'd been trying to help. It wouldn't have hurt him to listen to what she had to say, thank her for her thoughtful suggestions, then put the matter aside.

He sat up straight and took the drink she handed him. "You know, the roof repairs wouldn't have been such a royal pain in the butt if I hadn't spent so much time thinking about our little disagreement." It had been a disastrous afternoon. He'd dropped a hammer on Ben's foot and nearly whacked his head wrangler in the jaw with a two-by-four plank. Ben had finally told him he was more hindrance than help and to go away and let them finish the job.

He'd gone to the barn and spent a couple of hours trying to think through the problem. He eventually came to the conclusion that he was attempting to put some emotional distance between Samantha and himself. He had no alternative but to admit to himself that the prospect of where they were headed frightened him. The uncertainty frightened him. It had started out as a purely physical attraction, but he couldn't deny that it was slowly encompassing a growing emotional involvement as well. That was what frightened him the most.

"I thought a lot about it, too." The tension that had been churning in the pit of her stomach all afternoon vanished as soon as she saw his smile. "I owe you an apology. I had no right to—"

He grabbed her hand and pulled her down into his lap. "Let's forget it ever happened." He clinked the edge of his glass against hers. "Friends again?"

"Yes, friends again."

As it had the night before, the evening settled into a warm familiarity. Following dinner, they once again found themselves stretched out on the floor pillows in the living room in front of the fireplace. But there the similarity stopped. Any doubts or indecision that previously existed had since been cast aside.

Jace pulled her on top of him. His mouth held hers captive, hungrily demanding what she willingly gave. Their tongues explored as if they had a life of their own—each tasting, seeking.

He worked one of his hands inside the back of her jeans. His fingers caressed the silky fabric of her panties where they covered the curve of her seat. His actions were at first tentative but then became more confident. He felt her tremble, but in no way did she offer any hesitation. If anything, her ardor increased with the in-

timate gesture. His arousal strained against the fabric of
his jeans, the denim tautly stretched in an effort to con-
tain his hardened desire.

He momentarily relinquished his claim on her mouth
so he could cover her face with kisses. He started with
her nose, then moved to her forehead and worked his
way over to her ear. He nuzzled his face into the side
of her neck and whispered breathlessly, "Yesterday you
pulled away from me. I was afraid I'd been too aggressive, done something to offend you. Tonight you're everything a man could want. You seem to be an enigma
wrapped inside a puzzle—a paradox."

He pulled back just far enough to take in the flushed
excitement of her face, the burning passion in her eyes,
the kiss-swollen lushness of her mouth. "There's an aura
surrounding you—something very beautiful yet just out
of reach, like a sparkling diamond with a sign that says
look but don't touch. But at the same time there's an
earthy sensuality about you that could melt the polar ice
cap. Which one are you, Samantha Burkett?"

He brushed a soft kiss across her lips. "I don't like
playing idle little games. I never have, and I'm too old
to start now. We're obviously from two different worlds,
and you'll be returning to yours as soon as this storm
lifts." He paused a moment as he tried to stare into her
soul. "But in the meantime, are you merely toying with
me? Is this just something to do to pass the time until
the storm clears and you're able to return to the big city
and your own lifestyle? Or do you feel what I'm feeling?
Something much more than just a simple flirtation or the
mechanics of sex."

"You have me so confused, I don't know what I'm
feeling. This has all been so fast, so—" She closed her
eyes for a moment, as if trying to compose herself. "All

I know is that no one has ever made me feel this way
before...ever. I don't like games, either. I'm no good at
them, never have been. You're right about us coming
from two different worlds. You have a ranch to run, and
I have a job that I need to return to. But this is no game
for me, Jace.''

A strange sensation forced its way into her consciousness—one that said getting back to her competitive business world, her silk, tailored suits, and her small, anti-
septic apartment were not necessarily such a desirable
thing. She didn't know where the feeling had come from,
but she did know that she was very unhappy with it.

All through their intimate exchange of honesty, his
hand had remained inside the back of her jeans, seduc-
tively stroking her curves. He ran his other hand beneath
the back of her sweater, coming to rest on the single
hook holding her bra closed. She felt his fingers working
at the hook. She was also acutely aware of his erection
pressing against her leg. Every move he made, every
breath he took, telegraphed waves of sensual longing
through her body. Nothing and no one had ever tapped
into the very core of her existence the way he had.

Her bra hook gave way. Jace rolled her over on her
back, partially covering her body with his. He cupped
her bare breast in the hollow of his hand. His touch
heated more than her senses and desires. It warmed directly to her heart. Never before had anyone so totally
overwhelmed her the way Jace Tremayne had with nothing more than a caress. She slipped her hands under his
shirt and skimmed her fingers across the tensed muscles
of his back.

Her hardened nipple tickled against his palm, teasing
his senses. He pushed up her sweater until he had ex-
posed her breasts, then smothered her with kisses—her

face, her neck, her throat—finally arriving at the delectable treat. He laved the succulent flesh with the flat of his tongue before finally drawing her nipple into the moist warmth of his mouth.

An audible sigh escaped her throat, a sound that matched his own deep sense of pleasure. She arched her back, forcing her body even closer to his, if that were possible. While she continued to stroke his tautly muscled shoulders and back with one hand, she eased her other hand across her stomach until she could reach the front of his shirt. She fumbled with the buttons, trying her best to undo them.

But somewhere in the back of Samantha's perception was a nagging little bit of reality that tried to fight its way through a sea of euphoria. As much as she wanted to make love with Jace, she had to put a stop to what was happening, at least for now...while she was still able.

"Jace?" Her breathless whisper faltered as she tried to get control. His only response was a soft moan as he kissed the underside of her breast, then moved to suckle her other nipple.

Her mind began to clear as the importance of her concern crystallized. "Jace..." Her voice took on an edge of authority. She shook his shoulder and tried to sit up. "Jace...listen to me. Before it's too late...before things get totally out of hand..."

He freed her nipple, pausing long enough to tease the delightful mouthful with his tongue one last time before finally releasing it. He cupped the underside of her breast in his hand and bestowed a soft kiss on it. He furrowed his brow in concentration as he tried to focus on what she was saying. "Too late? What do you mean? Too late for what?"

She closed her eyes and wrapped her arms around his neck. "We...we need to talk. We're about to take a major step. And...well, there're certain things that need to be considered...brought out into the open..."

He still didn't understand what she was trying to say. He shook his head in confusion. "You want to *talk?* You've picked this moment to have a conversation?" He propped himself up on one elbow and stared at her. Then he saw the genuine concern on her face.

He immediately sat upright, reached out and gently caressed her cheek. "What's wrong, Samantha? Have I done something?" He moved his fingers under her chin and gently lifted until he could see all of her face. "We're adults, and we both know this isn't a permanent situation." He paused for a moment, furrowing his brow as if pondering something. "You'll be leaving, returning to your home in Los Angeles...." He searched her eyes for a moment, not really sure what he was looking for. His words trailed off, his voice becoming soft almost to the point of exposing the very real anxiety that thought caused him. "Not that I'm particularly happy about it, but I do understand that you have your job, your life—"

"Yes, my life and my world," she said with disdain. She grasped his hand, then laced their fingers together. She looked at the contrast of his tanned skin twined with her much paler coloring. One more defining difference between their worlds. She shook away the uncomfortable thoughts. "It's...well..." She glanced down then quickly regained eye contact with him. "Before things get totally out of control I think we need to talk about birth control and safe sex."

Jace took a deep breath, then slowly expelled it before wrapping her in a warm embrace. It had been a long time since the need for birth control or safe sex had been

a consideration for him. He and Stephanie had been together for three years, then married for two. It had been
nine years total since he had been involved in the dating
circus. Her concern told him she did not take the subject
lightly.

He took another steadying breath. "You're right. It's
a matter that needs to be addressed."

She felt awkward asking, but it had to be done. This
was the time for adult maturity, not immature embarrassment. "Do...uh...do you have any condoms?"

"No." He could not hide the disappointment that
rushed in to replace the excitement of a few minutes
earlier.

Regardless of how much they wanted to indulge the
physical pull between them, it would have to wait. They
would not make love tonight. He held her closely and
stroked her hair as he tried to calm his very real state of
arousal.

Jace stepped out onto the front porch, his coffee mug
in his hand. He took a large swallow, immediately followed by another. He needed the caffeine kick. He had
spent a very bad night. He'd tossed and turned for hours
before falling into a restless sleep. At one point he had
even thought about going to the bunkhouse to see if
anyone there had any condoms, but just as quickly dismissed it as a terrible idea. What he and Samantha did
in private was no one else's business. He had no right
to make her the object of bunkhouse amusement and
gossip, even though his every thought and every nuance
of his being cried out for her touch.

The snowfall continued, but the wind had died down
considerably. He watched as the Sno-Cat pulled out of
the large garage facility that housed all the ranch's ve-

hicles. It appeared that Vince had decided to make the run to get Samantha's suitcase. It was an encouraging sign. If things stayed relatively calm for a few hours, maybe he would be able to get into town to the drugstore. Maybe the helicopter—

"Good morning."

Jace whirled around. He'd been so absorbed in his thoughts he hadn't heard her come out the door. The moment he saw her, a gush of emotion flooded through him. He flashed a warm smile and held out his hand toward her. "Good morning." He immediately grasped her hand in his as soon as she stepped close enough. "Did you sleep well?"

She returned his smile. Sleep well, indeed! She doubted she'd had over three hours sleep, total. "Fine, and you?"

"Oh, just fine." He leaned forward and brushed a quick kiss across her lips. A mischievous grin tugged at the corners of his mouth. "Best night's sleep I've had in years, except for all the hours I spent tossing and turning, staring through the darkness at the ceiling and pounding my pillow into about fifty different shapes."

The smile faded from his face, leaving behind a serious expression. He placed his fingertips beneath her chin and lifted until he could look directly into her eyes. "And in between each toss and turn I thought a great deal about you...about us."

His words sent a thrill tingling through her body, and the silvery depths of his eyes held her to him as strongly as if he had wrapped her in his embrace. Her voice came out as a breathless whisper. "What thoughts about us?"

"Lots of thoughts." An uninvited huskiness crept into his voice. "Like what today holds in store...and more important, tonight." He hesitated a moment, knowing he was about to enter uncertain territory. "Like what's going to happen when this storm clears and the roads are open again."

Did he dare say more? "Thoughts about my having initiated unprotected...not even giving a thought to my responsibility with birth—" He glanced off toward the horizon for a moment, then returned his attention to her. "It's just that it's been so long since I...well, I guess taking precautions didn't occur to me." He glanced down at the wooden planking on the porch. The indecision welled inside him. He quickly swallowed it. "I guess it wasn't exactly my head that was doing my thinking," he said quietly and with emotion.

He placed his hands on her shoulders. He saw the look cross her face, the one that said she wasn't sure how to respond to what he'd just said. He forged ahead, not really certain where the conversation would lead. "I felt something between us, something more than my desire to make love to you all night long." He dropped his hands to his sides. A barely audible sigh escaped his lips. "I guess I just wanted us to share that."

Samantha could not ignore the apprehension he exhibited or the nervous way his silver eyes continued to search her face. She was not sure how to answer him. But as for that something special he'd mentioned, she knew it was true for her, as well. There was no way she could deny it, but she was unsure about how to handle it. She needed time to think, to analyze, to look at all facets of the situation. "Jace..."

He heard the hesitation in her voice and felt the immediate pang of disappointment it produced inside him. He had gone too far—said more than he had any right to, more than he wanted to. He forced a smile and changed the subject before she had an opportunity to say something that he feared would jab a wound into his heart.

"Well, I think we'd better get inside where it's warm." He held the door open for her. "How about some breakfast? Do you think you can handle fixing the eggs and toast while I do some bacon? After that I need to get busy...take advantage of this momentary break in the wind."

He kept up the idle chitchat all during breakfast effectively preventing the conversation from turning to *real* matters. He felt awkward. He had an overwhelming need to get out of the house, to involve himself in some type of physical labor that would require all his energy. Anything to get away from the magnetic pull she seemed to be effortlessly exerting on him without even realizing it.

He pushed back from the table as he drained the last swallow of coffee from the mug. He avoided making eye contact with her because he was too uncomfortable to meet her questioning gaze.

"I...uh...have a pretty busy schedule. I'll just grab lunch with the guys at the bunkhouse." He glanced out the window in an elaborate pretense at watching the falling snow. "Why don't you stay inside today? No sense in both of us going out in this." He nervously cleared his throat. "I'll see you later."

Samantha watched in silence as Jace left the house. She'd heard what he'd said, and she was sure she knew what he really meant. He was telling her she was in the way, that she caused him problems and made extra work for him, rather than being helpful. It upset her that he thought of her as an incompetent woman who was only in the way. It bothered her because she was not accustomed to failing when she set out to perform a task. But it bothered her even more because it was Jace Tremayne who thought it. She wasn't sure what to do about the problem. She would have to think about it and to come up with a logical solution.

In the meantime she needed to make a phone call. It had been a week since she left Los Angeles, and she had not once checked her answering machine for messages. She went to the den where she'd seen a speaker phone. She found a piece of paper and a pencil, then dialed her home phone number. After her machine answered, she punched in the code number that played back her messages. She was surprised to hear she had eight messages. She listened on the speaker and made notes. It was a string of unimportant matters, things that could wait. She continued to listen.

Jace had only gotten halfway across the yard when he realized he had left his watch in the bedroom. He turned and went back to get it. As he walked down the hallway he heard an unfamiliar voice coming from the den. He paused at the doorway and saw Samantha collecting phone messages. He continued on to his bedroom, retrieved his watch and headed back toward the front door.

He paused at the door of the den and started to say something to her when a male voice came from the phone's speaker. He saw her tremble, then hug her shoulders as if she were cold. She stared at the phone. The voice on the speaker contained a decidedly nervous edge.

"Samantha...are you home? Pick up the phone." There was a pause, then the voice continued. "Well... uh...I guess we need to talk. I waited for you to come back. Uh...well, call me when you get home. Well, actually...I'm about to go out. Call me in the morning. We'll talk about this." The click of the receiver was followed by the answering machine's computerized voice giving the date and time of the call.

A hard knot of anger formed in the pit of Jace's stomach. The caller was obviously her ex-fiancé and he had only made the call the previous evening. What had he been doing all those days since he'd seen her? He hadn't even been concerned enough to call right away in an attempt to find out if she'd gone home, if she was all right.

Jace wasn't sure how to handle what he'd inadvertently overheard. Should he go to her? Comfort her? Or would that only embarrass her, make her feel that he'd invaded her privacy by listening to her phone message even though it was unintentional? He finally decided it would be best to pretend that he hadn't heard. He left without her knowing he'd returned to the house, but the phone message ran over and over in his mind as he stepped out onto the front porch. How was it possible for her to have been engaged to such a man?

Samantha sat in the chair, staring at the phone. It had been a week since she'd surprised Jerry. A week since she'd turned and walked away without him making any effort to stop her. A week before he'd even bothered to phone her. If there had been any lingering doubts in her mind, they'd just been banished forever. There was no reason to return the phone call. They had nothing to say to each other. That episode of her life was over for good. Even though she'd known things between them were finished, it had taken his phone call to give her the closure she needed.

Samantha took a deep breath, held it a moment, then slowly exhaled. She rose from the chair, stood up straight and squared her shoulders. A slight smile tugged at the corners of her mouth. It was as if a huge weight had been lifted from her shoulders, setting her free.

She was now more determined than ever to prove to Jace that she was not a liability, a klutz who created havoc and left a trail of disaster in her wake. There had to be something she could do. It was obvious he didn't want her around the chickens again. She furrowed her brow in concentration as she returned to the kitchen. She mulled the problem over in her mind as she did the breakfast dishes. By the time the kitchen was clean she had an idea, but it would involve Ben Downey's help.

Just as she stepped out onto the porch she saw a large snow tractor type of vehicle pull into the garage. She noticed Jace following behind, then closing the big sliding door. She looked toward the bunkhouse where she hoped to find Ben. She turned up the collar on her heavy jacket, stuck her hands in the pockets and hurried across the yard.

She knocked at the bunkhouse door. When she received no answer, she tentatively opened the door a crack and called his name, not wanting to burst into the men's living quarters unannounced. "Ben...Ben Downey. Are you in here? It's Samantha."

"Yeah...be right out." Ben's voice came from down the hallway. A moment later he appeared. "Good morning, ma'am. Is there something I can do for you?" He motioned her inside, then shut the door behind her.

She glanced around the room, then promptly turned her attention to the purpose of her visit. "If you have some free time, I'd appreciate it if you could help me with something. It's a personal matter."

Curiosity immediately darted across his face. "Do you want to sit down?" He indicated a chair. "Now, what can I help you with?"

"Well, it's..." She suddenly felt very foolish. "Oh, it's too silly." She rose and prepared to leave. "I shouldn't have bothered you."

"Hold on, ma'am." Ben reached out and caught her arm. "You must have come here for a reason. What is it you need?"

She paused a moment, then bravely plunged ahead with her request, hoping it didn't sound as ridiculous as she knew it did. "I was wondering if you could...uh..." She glanced down at the floor then back at Ben. "Teach me how to milk a cow."

Ben Downey's eyes widened in shock. "Milk a cow?"

"Yes." Samantha tried to sound as confident about her request as possible, even though it bore no resemblance to the anxiety she felt.

His confusion showed and on his face. "Beggin' your pardon, ma'am, but why in the world would you want to learn how to milk a cow?"

"I thought it would be—" She paused for a moment, wrinkling her brow in concentration as she searched for just the right word, something that would sound plausible without giving away her true purpose. She brightened when it occurred to her. "*Educational.* As long as I'm here I thought I'd take advantage of the situation. I don't really know anything about ranch life and this seemed to be a great opportunity to learn."

"Well..." Ben ran his fingers through his hair to brush it back from his forehead. "I guess it won't hurt none. Did you check with Jace about this?"

Seven

"No, I didn't ask Jace. He seemed..." Samantha had not anticipated Ben's question. "Well, he seemed very busy. I didn't want to bother him with such a trifle."

She noted the frown that creased Ben's forehead. She moved quickly to relieve his worry by lowering her voice and injecting a conspiratorial tone. "To tell you the truth, I wanted to surprise him. We've had a couple of disagreements about city life versus country life, and I'm afraid I've left him with the impression that...well, let's just say we've had a couple of disagreements."

A wide grin spread across Ben's face. "Yes, ma'am. I believe I walked in on one of those disagreements." He grabbed his coat, hat and gloves. "I have some time right now, if this is good for you."

Samantha beamed her gratitude. "Now would be great."

They hurried to the barn. Samantha was filled with an

odd combination of enthusiasm and apprehension. She was not at all sure she was doing the right thing, but it was too late to back out.

"Now, this here's Emmylou." Ben gave the black-and-white cow a friendly pat on the rump. "She's a Holstein, one of two dairy cows we keep just to supply the ranch's needs." Then he added, almost as if it were an afterthought, "It's like the chickens. We just have enough of them to keep from having to buy eggs."

Her body stiffened at his mention of the chickens. She angrily muttered under her breath, "I know about the damn chickens." Unfortunately her words were louder than she'd intended.

Ben looked at her quizzically. "Pardon me, ma'am? Is there something wrong?"

She felt the flush of embarrassment creep across her cheeks. "No...nothing's wrong."

An awkward silence filled the air as Ben continued to stare at her. Samantha tried to recover by extending a warm smile. "So...where do we begin?" She looked around. "I don't see any of those milking machines. Where do you keep them?"

Ben's uninhibited outburst of laughter filled the air. It took a full sixty seconds for him to regain his composure while Samantha looked on in total bewilderment.

"Pardon me, ma'am. Didn't mean to bust out like that. It's just the idea of a milking machine...it kinda tickled my funny bone. For only two cows it's just as quick and easy to do it the tried and true way—by hand."

She swallowed hard. Had she heard him correctly? "You do all the milking by *hand?*" She definitely had not bargained for this.

While Samantha was learning about dairy cows, Jace

had other things on his mind. He barged into the garage
just as Vince was shutting down the Sno-Cat.

"How's it look out there, Vince?"

The tall, taciturn man in his early fifties climbed out
of the tractor cab, then pulled off his gloves before answering. "Some trees down. Bad drifts across the road.
Wind's picking up again. Snow coming down heavier.
Good chance the power lines could go down." He
reached inside the cab and pulled out a suitcase, a purse
and a set of car keys. He handed them to Jace, then
busied himself cleaning the wet, dirty vehicle. As usual,
his face registered no thoughts or feelings about the subject.

Jace took Samantha's belongings and hurried to the
ranch house. He envisioned the pleasure on her face
when he handed her the suitcase. With that thought in
mind, he burst through the front door, pausing only to
stomp the snow from his boots. Then he became aware
of the quiet. He listened for a moment. No radio, no
television, no noise coming from the kitchen or the den.
He took a few steps down the hallway. The door to the
guest room stood open, and the room appeared empty.

"Samantha?" He waited, but there was no answer.
He tried again. "Samantha, are you here?" Again, no
answer. He carried her things into the guest room and
set them on the bed, then he wandered back to the living
room. He could not imagine where she'd gone. Perhaps
the laundry room. He checked, but that room was empty,
too.

He instinctively whirled around and stared at the front
door. Not the henhouse again. Surely she had not made
yet another futile attempt to conquer the chickens, resulting in more broken eggs. She was a fish out of water,
a city girl lost in the country without a clue about how

anything functioned. She was also a fascinating and desirable woman who occupied more and more of his thoughts with each passing minute—thoughts that had been expanding to include an awareness of disturbing emotional feelings that had been making themselves known despite his attempt to shut them out.

Without making a conscious decision, he found himself headed toward the henhouse. To his surprise he found only chickens. No sign of Samantha and thankfully no broken eggs. Now he was truly perplexed. As he wandered back through the barn the sound of a muffled conversation reached his ear. He recognized Ben Downey's voice along with Samantha's.

"I think you're going to be real good at this, ma'am. You're a natural. Now, just wrap your hand around here—"

"Don't you think, under the circumstances, that you could drop the *ma'am* and call me Samantha?"

Jace came to an abrupt halt. He fixated on the specific words that had captured his undivided attention. He did not know what to make of the snippet of conversation he'd heard.

"Now, just move over here and wrap your hand around…yeah, like that." Jace heard the enthusiasm in Ben's voice.

Samantha's initial reaction to touching the cow's udder was hesitant at best, but she was determined. She mentally dug in her heels and prepared to do what she needed to do. "Oh, my…" She let out a nervous little laugh. "That's not at all what I thought it would feel like."

Jace felt a strange uneasiness rapidly building inside him. He couldn't see what they were doing, but their conversation certainly sounded questionable, almost as if—

He started to call out to Ben, but stopped himself in time. Instead, he made his way through the barn toward the direction of the voices. He peered over the partition. Relief washed over him, followed by even more insistent feelings of foolishness and guilt.

He watched for a moment as Ben instructed Samantha in the fine art of milking a cow. She was seated on the little three-legged stool with her back toward him. Ben stood on the other side, facing in Jace's direction, although he was watching Samantha. Every time Emmylou swished her tail or took a step in one direction or the other, Samantha flinched. But unlike with the chickens, she held her ground. She reached under the cow, then a moment later Jace heard the familiar pinging sound as the stream of milk hit the bottom of the pail.

"Oh!" Her exclamation of surprise was genuine. "I did it!" The sound of another squirt hit the metal pail. "I think I've got it." Her excitement mounted. "I'm doing it right, aren't I, Ben?"

A very pleased expression covered Ben's face as he watched Samantha's tentative efforts become more positive. "You sure are. You're doing just fine."

Ben looked up, his expression changing to surprise when he spotted Jace watching them. Ben started to speak, but Jace shushed him before he could say anything. Jace didn't want Samantha to know he was there. She hadn't approached him about learning to milk a cow. It was obvious she didn't want him to know—due in great part to their earlier disagreements about her handling of the chickens, he supposed.

A warm spot began to form deep inside Jace. He stepped away from the partition and sat down on a bale

of hay. Even after her previous disastrous efforts, she
was still determined to learn to do some kind of ranch
chore. He closed his eyes and allowed the memory of
the previous evening to settle over him—the hard bud
of her nipple pressed into the palm of his hand, the taste
of that same nipple as he teased it with his tongue before
drawing it into his mouth. It was a memory he knew
would remain with him for a long time after she had
gone.

The sound of Ben's voice interrupted Jace's thoughts.
He stood up and peered over the partition again.

"Are you okay with this now, Samantha?" Ben
pulled on his gloves. "If you are, then I'll get on with
my work."

She made an effort to project more confidence than
she actually possessed. "I'll get along fine. When I've
finished with Emmylou, you want me to take this bucket
of milk to Denny at the bunkhouse, right?"

"Right. Denny will take care of it from there."

"What about the other cow? Doesn't she need to be
milked, too?"

Ben chuckled. "I think one cow is more than enough
for your first time. Maybe tomorrow." Ben shot a quick
glance toward Jace, then left.

As soon as Ben was out of sight Emmylou became
restless. She fidgeted back and forth, each movement
becoming more and more aggressive in nature. She
shook her head, seemingly showing her displeasure with
Samantha's inexperience.

Samantha didn't like the way things were going. She
glanced toward the barn door, hoping to catch sight of
Ben. What she saw was the barn door closing as he
stepped outside. Emmylou sidestepped and Samantha
had to jump up from the stool to keep from being

knocked over. Everything had been going so well, then suddenly the docile cow had turned on her.

Samantha mimicked Ben's earlier gesture and patted the cow on the rump, all the time keeping a wary eye on Emmylou's erratic movements. She tried to project a calm, confident tone of voice. "Settle down now. That's a good girl. I'm not going to hurt you." The thought immediately popped into her head and came out her mouth in an apprehensive whisper. "And please don't you hurt me, either."

The cow seemed to calm down a little. Samantha positioned herself on the little milk stool, gave the cow another reassuring pat, then reached underneath to resume her milking. After a couple of awkward minutes, she finally developed a rhythm. She was very pleased with herself and her accomplishment. She would have a full bucket of fresh milk to deliver to Denny.

Jace elected not to interrupt Samantha's concentration. He turned away, paused for a moment as he decided which project to tackle, then headed toward the feed storage.

Emmylou's loud bellow filled the air, followed closely by a crash and Samantha's scream. Jace dashed the length of the barn, arriving in time to see Samantha sprawled on the ground, milk spilled all over the front of her clothes. The milk stool rocked back and forth on its side, finally coming to rest beside the empty pail. Emmylou stood quietly by, the picture of innocence while chaos erupted around her.

Jace shoved his hat back from his forehead as he slowly shook his head in amusement, trying his best not to laugh. Unfortunately his best was not good enough. His laughter reverberated throughout the large barn, filling every corner and reaching to the rafters.

He held out his hand toward her as he tried to control his laughter. "You look as if you could use a little assistance. Here, let me help you up." He grabbed her hand and pulled her to her feet.

Samantha didn't know whether to be embarrassed or angry. It was a toss-up for a minute, then anger won out. She glared at him. "I fail to see what's so funny!" She held his amused silver-eyed gaze for as long as she could before looking away. She wiped at the milk splattered across her jacket, covering the front of her shirt and her jeans. Suddenly she felt his strong, yet surprisingly tender touch brush the dirt and straw from her back.

The laughter continued to surround his words. "Come on, let's get you back to the house so you can change out of those messy clothes." He took her arm and started toward the door.

"I'll thank you to unhand me!" She yanked her arm from his grasp. "I can find my own way back to the house." She turned on her heel and angrily stomped across the open space, quickly covering the distance to the barn door.

Jace watched as she disappeared through the door. He put away the bucket and stool, then went to see Ben.

"What was all that business about? What prompted it?"

"I don't know, Jace. She came to the bunkhouse looking specifically for me. Asked if I'd teach her how to milk a cow. Said she thought it would be educational and that she wanted to surprise you. Didn't seem to be no harm in it. I guess Emmylou didn't agree with my decision." A hint of a grin tugged at the corners of Ben's mouth. "You know how these females are...don't none of them like strange hands grabbing at 'em."

"Yeah, I guess you're right." Ben might have been

making a joke about the cow, but it was the previous night's intimacies with Samantha that occupied Jace's mind. Was that how she'd felt? As if strange hands were grabbing at her?

Ben continued in a more serious vein. "Samantha was real eager and looked like she was getting along okay, but I should have stayed with her—made sure she didn't run into any trouble."

Jace clamped his hand on Ben's shoulder. "Don't worry about it. You only lost a bucket of milk." He flashed a somewhat sheepish grin. "I wasn't as lucky. While she was under *my* supervision, she scattered feed all over the henhouse and broke a basket of eggs...on *two* separate occasions. Barnyard chores are definitely not her strong point."

Samantha tromped through the snow as fast as she could, a combination of anger and exasperation pushing her forward. When she reached the front porch of the house, she turned to see if Jace was following. She experienced a slight twinge of disappointment when he was nowhere in sight.

She paused inside the front door long enough to take off her coat and snow boots. Next would be her wet, sticky clothes. Then, as soon as she had cleaned up, she needed to find something to do to ease her boredom.

The events of the past couple of days had left her disheartened. It seemed that every time she tried to help, she just ended up causing someone else more work. Jace had even tactfully *suggested* that she might be more comfortable if she stayed inside. Obviously he considered her a major liability and was attempting to keep her out of everyone's way.

She was accustomed to being active, but here on the

ranch it was different. Everyone seemed to be very busy, everyone had a job—everyone except her. Daytime television didn't interest her. She had tried on several occasions to sit down and read, but had been too restless to stay with it more than an hour or so at a stretch. She heaved a dejected sigh as she slowly walked to her bedroom to change her clothes.

Samantha stood in stunned silence. There, in the middle of the bed, sat her suitcase. How…when…she was having difficulty grasping it all. Somehow Jace had found a way of getting to her car and retrieving her belongings. One insignificant suitcase containing a week's worth of clothes—it was a small item in the overall scheme of things, but it meant a great deal to her. Having a few of her own possessions added a familiar comfort to her surroundings. Knowing that Jace had been responsible for the caring gesture gave her a warm feeling that suffused every corner of her body.

She quickly changed out of her milk-covered clothes, then turned her attention to her suitcase. She opened it and removed the contents. The clothes appeared unkempt from having been packed for so long. She ironed out the wrinkles and hung various articles of clothing in the closet and placed the rest in the dresser drawer. Next, she put her makeup and toiletries in the bathroom.

Her compulsive nature dictated that she always plan ahead, that she was always prepared, and she had packed her suitcase accordingly. It was a trait that, over the years, had proven to be a curse sometimes and a blessing at others. She smiled as she removed the final item from her suitcase and placed it in the dresser drawer. It had never been more of a blessing than it was now.

Jace stepped out of the shower and grabbed the towel from the rack. It had been a long day that had been made even longer by his determined effort to stay away from the house. He'd eaten both lunch and dinner at the bunkhouse, and in between he'd helped with the necessary repairs and cleanup from the first wave of the storm.

According to the weather forecast, by early evening they would be seeing the return of strong winds with increased snowfall. The forecast had been correct. The storm had resumed in all its fury. If Vince's prediction had any validity the power lines would be down before the night was through. If the power went, then that would also knock out the furnace. He laid the firewood in the fireplace in his bedroom in preparation for that eventuality.

Now he stood just inside his bedroom door. He hadn't bothered with any shoes, dressing only in jeans, a loose-fitting sweatshirt and socks. He reached for the doorknob, then hesitated a moment. Anxiety jittered in the pit of his stomach. He was concerned about the rest of the night, about where it might lead in spite of the brief conversation with Samantha concerning the pitfalls of intimacy. He took a calming breath, then opened the door. He couldn't avoid Samantha any longer or the direction his feelings for her seemed to be taking him.

As he walked down the hall he noticed the light shining from under her closed bedroom door. Perhaps she, too, had thought it best to maintain some distance between them. Even with the furnace on there seemed to be a chill in the air. He continued on to the living room where he built a fire in the fireplace. He turned on some soft music, then plopped into his favorite chair. Leaning back, he closed his eyes, his thoughts on Samantha.

Outside, a heavy blanket of fresh snow spread over the yard, burying everything even deeper. The wind howled around the eaves and whistled across the window casings. Inside, the logs crackled in the fireplace, and the flames radiated a sensual warmth throughout the room. The atmosphere was ripe for seduction, a possibility that continued to assault his senses in spite of his attempt to push it away. He knew he couldn't handle the frustration of another evening of starting something that couldn't be finished.

He knew something else, too. He knew that his attraction to Samantha had moved beyond the purely physical. He couldn't keep his thoughts away from her for more that a few minutes at a time. And they were thoughts of a personal nature that had nothing to do with making love. What were her favorite foods? Her favorite movie? What type of books did she enjoy? Did she have any interest in a family of her own?

"Good evening."

The sound of Samantha's voice jerked him out of his reverie. He looked up to see a vision standing by the large stone fireplace...a vision that totally captured his senses and almost took his breath away. Her hair looked different from the way she'd worn it since her arrival; it seemed fuller. The chestnut tresses feathered softly around her face, but with some curl to them. Her tastefully applied makeup accentuated her delicately sculpted features. The russet color that dotted her lips gave her mouth a lush appearance. The skirt of her emerald green dress fell to mid knee, revealing shapely calves and slim ankles. Her high heels matched the green color of her dress. The scooped neckline showed a hint of cleavage, just enough to be enticing without being too revealing.

"Good evening to you, too." He rose from his chair. A long, low whistle escaped his lips as his gaze slowly traced every line of her body from her face all the way down to the floor and back to her face. His words came out in a husky rush. "You look gorgeous!"

"Thank you." She felt the flush spread across her cheeks. She slowly crossed the room to where he stood.

"What prompted you to dress up?"

"I've been wearing jeans since I arrived. I thought a dress would be nice for a change…now that I have something to change into."

"You look like someone should be taking you out for the evening—wining and dining you in some elegant restaurant." He tentatively reached out to touch her hair, but withdrew his hand before making contact. "And if the weather didn't have us trapped here, that's exactly what I'd be doing."

She paused as if uncertain about whether or not to say something, then proceeded. "And if it weren't for the weather I wouldn't be here at all."

His expression turned deadly serious. "In that case I'll have to send the weatherman a thank you note for providing this storm."

A hint of anxiety tickled inside her. She'd spent the afternoon trying to convince herself that they were just too opposite for anything beyond the physical to ever come of the situation, but she hadn't been able to convince herself. She forced away the feeling and the recurring thought.

"Speaking of thanking someone, I'd like to thank you for rescuing my suitcase. That was so thoughtful. I can't begin to tell you how much it means to me to have my belongings. I know it sounds silly being so concerned with material possessions…" She glanced down at the floor for a second, then regained eye contact with him. "It's just clothes and a few personal items, but having them makes me feel so much better, so much more comfortable..." Her voice trailed off as the emotion welled inside her. "Not so isolated and alone."

He took her hand in his and pressed it to his lips. As much as he tried to fight the emotion, it refused to go away. "I'm sorry you've been so uncomfortable."

Her eyes widened in surprise. "Oh! I didn't mean to imply that it was your fault. You've been more than kind and gracious. You've gone out of your way to make me as comfortable as possible. It's just that...well, being in a strange place and—"

"I know." He pulled her to him and wrapped her in his embrace. "I know it's been difficult for you, and I know you've tried to help. And, just to keep the record straight, it was Vince who actually braved the elements and rescued your belongings."

"I'll have to make it a point to thank him in the morning, but I'm sure it wasn't his idea." Once again his silver-eyed gaze seemed to be stripping her soul bare. She felt a shortness of breath that she tried to ignore. "I'm sure...you must have sent him to do it."

Something else was obvious to her, too. If Vince had been able to get to her car, then he probably would have been able to get to other places, too. He could have taken her off the ranch and let her check into a motel in town. It might even have been possible for Jace to fly her out in the helicopter the same way he'd brought her in, but Jace hadn't approached her with either option. Instead, he chose to instruct Vince to retrieve her suitcase. She was glad. Had she known, it would have forced her to make a decision.

She didn't know whether she could have made that decision. It would have meant making a choice between the logical thing to do and what her heart wanted. And as much as she tried to deny it, her involvement with

Jace Tremayne had taken a very personal turn that exceeded the mere physical by leaps and bounds.

"Did I tell you how beautiful you look?" He continued to hold her against his body, savoring the sensation of the rise and fall of her breasts with each breath she took.

"Yes…" He had such an intoxicating effect on her that she found it difficult to speak. She found it equally difficult to think straight.

Before she could say anything else, he covered her mouth with his. The earthiness of her response immediately filled him with the knowledge that he would not be satisfied until he had it all. He slid his hand across the back of her dress. It had been a long time since he'd enjoyed the tactile sensation of soft, silky fabric or inhaled the heady fragrance of a sexy perfume.

He sought out the irresistible texture of her tongue and the delectable taste that was hers alone. Once again he was perilously close to being overwhelmed by his desires. He broke the kiss, cradled her head against his shoulder, then took a calming breath. He finally achieved enough control that his voice sounded calm and authoritative. "I think it might be a good idea if we slowed this down a bit before things get out of hand. Like you said, there are lots of practical matters to consider…things we should—"

He couldn't finish the sentence. He didn't want to finish it. He couldn't be the sensible, logical, pragmatic, dispassionate type of man she apparently preferred. Those qualities certainly had their place and use, but not now. Not when he wanted to make love to her more than he had wanted anything for a very long time. He tried to focus his attention on something else—something other than the tantalizing scent of her perfume, the silky strands of her hair twined around his fingers, the warmth of her body pressed against his.

He continued to hold her, even though he knew if he had any sense at all he would release her, go directly to his room and shut himself in for the duration of the night—or better yet, for the duration of her stay at his ranch. From the force with which the storm had resumed its assault, it could well be several more days before things cleared enough for her to be able to leave.

He listened to the wind howling around the corners of the house. It seemed to blend with the background music from the stereo to create a mixture of sounds that were strangely appealing...the wild abandonment of the storm and the carefully constructed notes of the song. He was the storm and she was the song. Was it possible for the two extremes to blend as perfectly with people? He didn't have the opportunity to ponder it for more than a few seconds before he felt the tentative foray of her hand beneath the back of his sweatshirt. At that moment he knew without a doubt that his good intentions had just been shot to hell.

Samantha didn't know how to justify her actions as she trailed her fingertips across his bare back. She didn't have a nice, logical well-thought-out plan. She hadn't weighed the pros and cons of the situation, had not evaluated every aspect of the moment. She knew only that he made her feel like no one else ever had...a feeling she wished could last forever.

She felt his muscles tense up as if he were steeling himself against some unknown intrusion, then he immediately relaxed. He held her tighter. She felt so warm and protected, as if she had finally found the mythical happiness she had been searching for all her life—a man who set her passions on fire and also touched the depths of her soul in a way she had never known. She started to speak, her courage growing with each word.

"Jace...uh...now that I have my suitcase...I have—"

The lights flickered and the music seemed to sputter and crackle. Then it stopped completely, and the house was plunged into darkness except for the soft illumination from the fire.

Jace stroked her hair, then bent down and placed a tender kiss on her forehead. "Apparently the power lines have gone down. I can't say I'm even remotely surprised, the way the wind's been blowing. We have some emergency oil lamps in the kitchen. They're not really bright enough to read by, but they give enough light to see what you're doing." He still hadn't released her from his embrace. "I'll get one for you to put in your bedroom."

She drew her courage together. Now was the time. "I have something here." She heard the quaver in her voice, but knew it was too late to turn back. She reached into the pocket of her dress and withdrew the package she had removed from her suitcase earlier. She held it out to him.

Jace blinked a couple of times as he focused on the item in Samantha's hand. The light from the fireplace was just enough for him to see what she held. Were his eyes playing tricks on him? Had his desires finally overwhelmed reality to the point where he was imagining things? He took the object from her, then turned it over several times in his fingers.

He looked at her questioningly. He couldn't hide the surprise in his voice as he looked at the package in his hand, then at her again. "Where in the world did you find these?"

Eight

Samantha quickly glanced down at the floor, her words cloaked in sudden embarrassment. "I had them in my suitcase. I mean...I was going to visit my fiancé... and...uh...well, I do have this thing about being prepared, so when I packed my suitcase..."

A smile of delight tugged at the corners of Jace's mouth, but he forced it away. Something other than the obvious pleasures indicated by the presence of the package popped into his thoughts. Had she felt pressured by him? Had he put her into a position where she felt she had no other recourse? He placed his hands on her shoulders and fixed her with a serious look, the package still clutched between his fingers. "I think some serious conversation is in order."

Panic welled inside Samantha. She'd been afraid of this, afraid he would be put off by her aggressive behavior. As much as she liked to think of herself as a liberated woman, it was not proper for her to initiate making love with someone, especially when that person was practically a stranger...no matter how much he made her blood race through her veins. Or how much she felt herself drawn to him on an emotional level.

She was accustomed to being in charge where business concerns were the order of the day, but this was not business. And Jace Tremayne was certainly not the type of man she normally came in contact with. He was a rancher, a cowboy who had already shown her that he had some strong opinions about a woman's place in his scheme of things. He was nothing like the type of man she had previously been involved with, the type of man with whom she was often in competition in the workplace.

Jace lived in a world so totally different from hers. There was no way she could ever be in competition with him. Had that been what had always gone wrong before? Had her push to compete and succeed been the destructive force in her relationships? So many self-searching thoughts had surfaced during the time she'd been stranded at the ranch...thoughts that made her uncomfortable. And thoughts that forced her to think about things she would rather avoid, such as whether she could ever fit into Jace's lifestyle. And now Jace was about to throw those thoughts and feelings in her face.

She pulled away, humiliation quickly spreading through her consciousness. She stuck her hands in her pockets and stared at the floor, too embarrassed to look up at him. Her words were as much mumbled as spoken. "That's okay, you don't need to say any more. I was totally out of line. I had no right to do that. I'll just go to my room now. Maybe I could have one of those lamps—"

He pulled her into his embrace, then his mouth came down hard on hers. The heat of his passion seared straight through to the very core of her existence. It vaporized everything that might have stood in the way of her total surrender to whatever the night held. A door had just been opened that she knew could never be closed again. She slipped her arms around his neck. The hard length of his body pressed against hers, every plane, angle and curve fitting together as if they'd been made for each other. A moment later his tongue invaded the dark recess of her mouth.

Jace easily picked her up, just as he'd done that fateful day when he spotted her from his helicopter. Only this time he didn't sling her across his shoulder. He cradled her gently in his arms and carried her down the hallway toward his bedroom. The power outage presented no problem, the darkness didn't offer any hindrance. This time there were no obstacles in the way, nothing to prevent them from making love. He put her down next to his bed, then reached through the dark to place the package on the nightstand.

Samantha trembled, not from the storm that raged outside, not from the darkness, not even from the sudden chill that permeated the air as a result of the furnace going out when power was lost. She trembled from pure excitement and sweet anticipation. The moment he scooped her up in his arms, her insides began to quiver, her heartbeat jumped into double time, and a warm sense of euphoria suffused her. If Jace's kisses were any indication of what was yet to be, then it would surely be the most exciting night of her life.

His arms were around her, his lips so close that his whispered words tickled across her ear. "Are you sure,

Samantha? I want to make love to you so much, but not if you don't want it as much as I do.''

His fingers found the tab at the neckline of her dress and a moment later she felt the cool air hit her bare skin as the zipper slid down her back. "You're stranded here until the storm lifts,'' he whispered huskily. *And after that you'll be leaving.* It was a thought that kept repeating, each time more distasteful than the last. "I don't want to put pressure on you to do something you don't really want." He tugged the dress fabric away from her shoulder, then brushed his lips against her skin. "Making love is something done by two willing people, not something imposed on someone who has doubts."

She slipped her arms around his waist, then up under the back of his sweatshirt. His muscles tensed when she ran her fingertips across his bare skin, and his arms tightened around her. Her voice held a confidence that she had not anticipated. "I don't have any doubts…no doubts at all."

Her dress fell to the floor. He stepped behind her so he could unhook her bra. It, too, fell to the floor. A little shiver of delight puckered her nipples into taut peaks. He reached his arms around her, cupping the fullness of her breasts in his hands as he kissed her nape. She placed her hands on top of his and closed her eyes, savoring each and every intimate gesture.

She leaned back against his body, her bare skin snuggled next to his clothes. She felt his arousal strain against his jeans, the hardness growing until it pressed firmly into the small of her back. She turned in his embrace until they stood face-to-face. Even in the darkness she could see the shimmer of his silver eyes, the glow of his desire. It matched the heat building inside her.

Jace skimmed his hands across her bare back. Her skin

emulated the silky smoothness of the fabric that had covered her just a breath earlier. It had been a long time since he'd allowed himself the intimate closeness of a desirable woman. He hadn't been ready to once again put his emotions on the line.

He wanted to take things slow with Samantha, to thoroughly experience the joy as they achieved each new level of intimacy on their way to the ultimate rapture. That was what he wanted, but he didn't know if it would be possible. Just touching her excited him to the point where he didn't know how long he would be able to maintain his control.

His hand caught the waistband of her panty hose and suddenly he was once again a teenage boy who was all thumbs and a mass of insecurities. "Do you think you could...I mean, would you mind handling your panty hose. I never—" He tried to stifle the embarrassed, awkward chuckle. "I never could deal with these things without disastrous results."

"No, I wouldn't mind." She kissed him on the cheek. This surprisingly shy demeanor seemed to take over his naturally forceful personality. It was such an endearing quality. No pretenses, no phoniness. He was not all slick moves and practiced sophistication. This dynamic and assertive man was so real. Everything about him was real...as real as her feelings for him.

With quick movements, almost frantic in nature, he pulled off his sweatshirt, jeans, socks and finally his briefs, while she wiggled out of the panty hose and dropped them on top of her dress.

The sound of their breathing did battle with the howling wind for control of the surrounding space. The chill in the room had long since been replaced by the incendiary passion that burned between them. He cupped her face in his hands and settled a tender kiss on her lips. The quaver in his voice gave away his nervousness, even though he tried to make the words sound light and casual. "Last chance to back out."

She ran her hands across his well muscled chest, then placed a soft kiss there. She felt his strong heartbeat when her lips touched his skin. "How about you...are you having second thoughts about this?"

His emphatic response was immediate. "No way." He captured her mouth before she could say anything more.

He lowered her body to his bed, then stretched his tall frame next to her. He had a tenuous grasp on his control at best. He cupped her breast in his hand, reveling in the feel of her tautly puckered flesh against his palm. He drew her other nipple into his mouth and held it there while teasing the hardened bud with the tip of his tongue. He suckled—at first gently, then with increased ardor. He was not sure whether the soft moan of pleasure had come from her or emanated from his own throat.

He ran his hand along the indentation of her waist and traced the flare of her hip, finally reaching the downy softness nestled between her thighs. His hand closed over the delicate folds of her femininity. The moist heat of her excitement touched him physically and enveloped him emotionally. She was everything he could possibly want or need.

Samantha had never experienced anything to match the thrill of Jace Tremayne's touch. She knew of no other way to express it than to say that he simply set her soul on fire. She ran her fingers through his thick blond hair before arching her back to bring herself more fully against his mouth. He responded to her cue by hungrily drawing in more of her breast. She caressed his strong shoulders and ran her fingers across his back.

He shifted his weight slightly, straddling her leg and placing his knee between her sleek thighs. She trailed her fingertips across his bottom cheek while running her foot along his calf. His muscles flexed and rippled beneath her touch, shooting little surges of excitement through her body. The tingling sensation settled low inside her, connecting with the deeply intense surge of pleasure when he inserted his finger between her feminine folds and brushed his thumb across the core of her sexual being.

He released her nipple from his mouth, trailed the tip of his tongue across the valley between her breasts, then quickly captured her other tautly drawn cap. He nibbled and tugged gently with his lips before taking her fully into his eager mouth.

She wrapped her arms around his head as the waves of euphoria built toward a throbbing crescendo. She shoved back into the pillow. Her mouth fell open, but no sound came out. She arched her hips upward, pushing hard against his hand. Everything seemed to move in sync—the way his mouth greedily possessed her breasts as if they were his own personal treasure, the intense stimulation from his busy fingers, the feel of bare skin rubbing against bare skin. It was an unrestrained oneness that totally enveloped both of them in the heat of the moment.

The rapture exploded, melting the words that had been frozen in her throat. "Jace...oh...I can't think straight...." She gulped for air, unable to say any more, as the convulsions reverberated deep inside her. A moment later his mouth was on hers.

This was a part of Jace's life he'd thought would

never be open to him again. Now, that had all changed.
A beautiful woman whom he found himself caring for
more deeply with each passing moment, perhaps too
deeply, writhed in ecstasy at his touch and called out his
name. The moment he had longed for, the moment he
had anticipated with overwhelming desire, was here—
but it was also a moment touched with a hint of anxiety.
Would he be able to please her? To fulfill her needs? It
was important to him, much more so than the physical
pleasure he would derive.

Jace reached out to the nightstand, groping around in
the dark until he located the package he'd placed there
earlier. He propped himself up on one elbow as he
tugged at the wrapper. Frustration churned inside him
when he couldn't get it open. "What's with this damn
thing? Is it welded shut?" He took a deep breath to force
a calm control to his actions, then tried again.

The wrapper finally gave way. A feeling of both triumph and relief came out as he spoke. "Got it." He tore
open the package and took out one of the individual
packets. Before he had a chance to rip it open, it was
lifted from his hand.

Had she changed her mind? Trepidation suddenly shot
through his body. Then he felt her hand skim across his
thigh followed by a sensual stroking of his manhood. A
low groan of intense pleasure eased its way out of his
throat.

"I...uh..." His heart pounded. Words were difficult
for him. "I thought for a moment there that you might
have reconsidered." Her hand was warm, her touch incredibly exciting. "And if you had changed your mind,
I think it just might have caused irreparable damage to
my psyche—" He could not stop his quick intake of
breath followed by a salacious growl of primal need

when she trailed the tip of her tongue lightly along the length of his erection.

Samantha could not believe her audacious behavior. Never before had she been so brazen in her actions, taking the initiative without thought as to whether something would be appropriate. With Jace, everything seemed so natural. She opened the packet and withdrew the contents. "Allow me." Her words were a husky whisper as she sheathed his manhood.

Jace covered her body with his. The strong thump of his pounding heart resonated through to her own hammering heartbeat. She wrapped her legs around his hips and sensually stroked his shoulders and back with an intense urgency. She reveled in the provocative way his tongue meshed with hers.

His manhood tentatively probed at her entrance, almost as if he were uncertain about proceeding. Then a forward thrust of his hips placed his rigid length deep inside her. Time stood still as they remained melded into one with neither of them moving—perhaps for a second or perhaps for several minutes, she didn't know.

Jace kissed the tender spot behind her ear, then sucked her earlobe into his mouth and held it there for an instant. His breath came hot and hard against her neck followed by words thick with emotion. "My God, Samantha...I had almost forgotten how unimaginably fantastic...you are so—" His mouth took charge, extracting her very essence, then demanding even more.

He moved his hips, coaxing her into a tantalizing rhythm that escalated in a frenzied rush toward the pinnacle. Neither of them seemed able to exert any control over their incendiary drive to reach that heady realm of ecstasy.

Once again the convulsions started deep inside her,

quickly engulfing her entire body in a delicious explosion. She grabbed at Jace, wanting to hold him even closer to her, if that were possible. No one in her entire life had ever transported her to the heights where Jace had just taken her. And she never wanted to come back down to earth.

His chest heaved and his heart pounded as he gave one final deep thrust. The spasms shook him in an eruption of cataclysmic proportions. A low, rumbling moan of intense pleasure was all he could manage until he caught his breath enough to say, "I think you've killed me." He gasped for air, barely getting out the words, "But it's one hell of a way to go." A second later his mouth was on hers—at first infusing her with the searing spasms that still lingered inside him, then settling into the warm familiarity produced in the wake of their passion.

The cold air finally took charge and dictated the next item on the agenda—that and his almost obsessive need to get some light into the room so he could see her. He had to be able to look into her face and her eyes, to know if they held pleasure or disappointment. Tenderly, he kissed each of her nipples before whispering in her ear, "I'd better start a fire in the fireplace." He again teased each hardened bud, this time with the tip of his tongue. It was as if he were unable to tear himself away. Finally he said, "I'll be right back."

He made his way through the dark to the fireplace. He struck a match and a nice blaze soon radiated its warmth across the room.

Samantha pulled the blanket up around her shoulders. She watched Jace move the logs around with the poker and stoke the fire to keep it burning for a long time. His tautly muscled, nude body glistened in the subdued light.

She had never in her entire life felt as totally satisfied as she did at that moment. It was more than being sexually fulfilled. It was a magical sense of calm, a type of contentment that had never before been part of her life—a contentment that had somehow eluded her...until now.

Jace climbed into bed, pulling the covers across both of them. He wasn't sure what to do, what Samantha expected of him or what she needed. He wanted so much to do the right thing, but he didn't know what that was. The glow from the fireplace reached across the room to the bed. He brushed back the tendrils of hair matted against her damp forehead, then enfolded her in his arms. The smile emanating from her face was not wide, not beaming, but it said far more than any words. It spoke of warmth, fulfillment, and radiated an inner peace that touched the depths of his very existence. The same pleasure shone in her eyes.

He pressed his lips against her forehead, taking enjoyment in the way her breasts seemed to nuzzle against his chest. He ran his hands down her back and cupped the roundness of her bottom, pulling her body hard against his. Never before had the mere touch of a woman's skin brushing against his sent a thrill coursing through him the way it was at that moment. But there was more. What he felt transcended the physical and went directly to the emotional core of his life.

His voice held more confidence than earlier. "Is there something you need, Samantha? Something you want? Is there anything I can do for you?" He relished the delicious shudder that passed through his body when she ran her foot along his calf, a shudder that flowed to his manhood with unexpected results. He felt the stirrings of his desire begin to pulsate and grow.

Samantha felt his arousal press against her. His excitement spread to her, infusing her with the same heated desire. She reached for him. She thought she had already attained the pinnacle of euphoria, been taken to heights beyond anything she had ever known. But as soon as her fingers came in contact with his rapidly hardening sex, her nerve endings galvanized into a tingling craving for more…much more.

He reached for her hand, gently pulling it away from his revived state of readiness. "I wouldn't do that if I were you." He nuzzled the side of her neck and whispered in her ear, "Unless you're serious."

She nipped playfully at his shoulder blade with her lips. "I wouldn't kid you about something this serious…." She teased the length of his manhood with her fingertips, then stroked and caressed his potency. "And this certainly seems very serious to me."

"Hmm…I'll be happy to show you just how serious I am. How many of those little packets do you have?"

"I think there's enough to handle as many times as you want to demonstrate your sincerity." Her words teased him as she wrapped her leg around his, but her voice and actions told him exactly how real those words were.

It had become too hot under the blanket, mostly from internal heat. He threw off the covering, then provocatively laved attention on her breasts with the flat of his tongue. He paused for a moment as he studied the way the glow from the fireplace highlighted her features and glistened on her wet nipples. "You're a very beautiful and desirable woman, Samantha Burkett."

His mind suddenly filled with all sorts of thoughts, not the least of which were his final moments with his wife. He recalled her last words as she lay dying in the emergency room of the hospital. *You have your entire life ahead of you. Please don't spend it alone. I want you to find happiness, someone to be with. I love you.* And with that she'd given his hand a weak squeeze and closed her eyes. A moment later she was gone.

The final stage of closure that had begun when he opened the trunk in search of some clothes for Samantha was now fully realized. He knew he could get on with his own life—with a new life. He kissed Samantha on the forehead and held her closely. He placed another soft kiss on her cheek. He could not imagine how her former fiancé could possibly want anyone else when he had her. The guy must have been a prime jerk. She was certainly better off without him. Jace knew he could take care of her, treat her the way she deserved to be treated, love her more than—

The uninvited thoughts had popped into his mind without warning. He quickly captured her mouth in an attempt to force them away. Things were moving too quickly. He had to keep the facts in mind. This was an incredibly delicious interlude to the surrounding chaos, a man-made storm in the middle of one created by nature. He didn't know how to confront the emotional side of what was happening. And with Samantha returning to her home as soon as the storm cleared, it might not happen at all.

Samantha watched Jace as he slept. She'd been awake for nearly half an hour, since the predawn tinge of gray had begun to alter the black of night. The fire had almost died out, so she slipped out of bed as quietly as possible and added a couple of logs to restore the flames. Then she hurried back to bed and slid under the covers.

She glanced at the nightstand where the three empty packets gave evidence of the passion that had exploded between them. Three times they had made love during the course of the night; three times he had proven to her how perfectly suited they were for each other...at least physically. She knew more than just the physical existed for her, in spite of the differences between them. But what about Jace? What did he feel? Her thoughts were interrupted when he rolled over and pulled her into his embrace.

His words were thick with sleep, his eyes still closed. "Are you awake?"

"Yes, I've been awake for a little while." She hadn't had that much sleep, yet she felt totally rested. "It was getting cold so I added some logs to the fire."

His eyes remained closed, but his actions were awake. He pulled her over, until her body rested on top of his. He whispered in her ear, "Maybe I could figure out some way to help you warm up." He ran his hands smoothly down her bare back until he firmly cupped the roundness of her bottom.

A shiver ran through her body, but it was not caused by the cold. She ran her fingers through his tousled hair and brushed a kiss against his lips. "I don't think there's any way you could get it any hotter in here than it was last night."

Jace finally opened his eyes. His words came out as a soft caress. "Last night..." He placed a gentle kiss at the corner of her mouth. "Last night was very important to me. Thank you for making it special."

A teasing grin tugged at the corners of her mouth. "Isn't that what the woman is supposed to say?"

"I guess that's true most of the time." His demeanor became serious as he traced her upper lip with the tip of his finger. Was she mocking him? He searched her eyes, trying to read whatever they held. What he found was warmth and honesty without a hint of any pretense. He brushed her hair back from her face then cupped her chin in his hand. "It's been a long time, Samantha."

The fact that he lived on a ranch rather than in town had not adversely affected the numerous opportunities presented to him—opportunities he had declined. He hadn't been ready to resume that part of his life...not until now, and not with anyone other than Samantha. "There hasn't been anyone in the four years since my wife died. I wasn't sure I would remember how—"

She placed her fingers against his lips to hush his words. Things sounded as if they were headed down a very serious path, and she didn't know if she was ready for that. She wanted to lighten the moment. "I guess it's like riding a bicycle, you never forget how."

He studied her for a moment, his brow wrinkled in concentration. "Are you going to be okay with this?"

A hint of puzzlement crossed her face. "Okay with it?"

"I mean, when you leave. When you return home." The words hurt even as he said them. He also knew he had to accept the reality of the situation. When the storm lifted, she would be gone.

"Oh." The utterance was flat, said without expression. She didn't want to think about returning home. Even though she knew it had to be, she did not want to think about it right now. "When I return home." She forced a weak smile.

"Hey, Jace..." Ben's voice came from the hallway. "Are you awake?" The sound drew closer.

Jace called out, hoping to stop him before he got any closer. "Yeah, Ben...I'll be there in a minute."

Jace threw back the cover and swung his legs over the edge of the bed. He grabbed his watch from the

nightstand and muttered more to himself than anyone,
"No wonder...I had no idea it was so late."

"Uh...I'll...uh...wait in the kitchen." Ben's voice
had suddenly taken on a different tone, an awkward hesitation that said he had become uncomfortable about
something.

Jace quickly pulled on some clothes, then leaned
across the bed toward Samantha. "I'm sorry about having to rush off like this. Apparently there's some emergency. Between the storm and the power lines going
down..." He brushed a soft kiss across her lips.
"There's no reason for you to be up this early. Why
don't you stay right here and go back to sleep?" He
didn't wait for an answer, but he leaned his face into
hers and placed another kiss, this time allowing his lips
to linger against hers for several seconds.

Jace left the bedroom, closing the door behind him.
As he walked down the hallway he realized what it was
that had caused Ben to suddenly sound so uncomfortable. The door to the guest room—Samantha's bedroom—stood wide open and the bed was still neatly
made. It was obvious that she was nowhere else in the
darkened house and that her bed had not been slept in.

He caught up with Ben at the front door. "What's the
problem? The generator kicked in okay, didn't it?" He
grabbed his hat and coat from the rack.

Ben's curious glance toward Samantha's bedroom did
not go unnoticed. Nor did the questioning way Ben
looked at him before speaking. "Vince had a devil of a
time keeping that generator going. Everything checked
out okay when he tested it a few days ago, but
now...well, I don't know. Vince will have to fill you
in." Ben opened the front door and stepped out onto the
front porch. "We've moved the newly hatched chicks

and the incubating eggs into the bunkhouse to keep them warm. They're okay for now."

"Sounds like you had a busy night. Did you get any sleep at all?"

"Well…" Ben jerked his head back toward the house. A little grin appeared, a combination of curiosity and an all-knowing amusement. "I probably got as much sleep as you did."

Ben and Helen both had provided the strong emotional support Jace needed immediately following the death of his wife. He knew he could never have kept the ranch running smoothly were it not for the way Ben had jumped in and literally taken over. He owed Ben a great deal, but he wasn't sure how much of an explanation he owed him about the previous night.

Jace chose to ignore the pointed statement. "Is the generator the only problem? Is the patch on the stable roof holding okay?"

Nine

Samantha stood at Jace's bedroom window with the bedspread wrapped around her. She watched as the two men crossed the yard in the early-morning light. Snow swirled in the air, but it seemed to be a result of the wind whipping it up from the ground rather than new snow falling. Even with the fireplace providing heat, the chill in the air sent a shiver across her bare skin. She pulled the bedspread tighter around her body as she crossed the room.

The idea of lolling around in Jace's bed, warm and secure beneath the blankets, appealed to her very much. She briefly entertained the thought of being able to stay for longer than the morning...maybe even forever. She shook the thought away as being totally impractical and illogical, but it still insisted on lingering in the back of her consciousness. She needed to turn her attention to more immediate matters.

She had been relieved to find that there was hot water even if the power outage had knocked the furnace out. As soon as she had showered and dressed, she headed for the kitchen. She began searching the cupboards for an old stove-top coffeepot and finally found one in the storage room.

While she waited for the coffee to perk she wandered aimlessly around the house, but kept returning to the same place—Jace Tremayne's bedroom. A warm feeling of contentment still lingered in the air, then welled inside her as she touched the rumpled sheets. She took in her surroundings with a critical eye, for the first time really looking at the personal items in his bedroom.

She was left with the impression of a hard-working man who possessed strength of character, honesty and integrity, combined with a sense of humor and fun. She recalled the spontaneous snowball fight, the pure enjoyment of something that had no purpose other than fun. There had been far too few of those moments in her life.

Then her gaze lit on the opened packets on the nightstand. She picked them up and threw them in the trash, then put the package they came from in the nightstand drawer. The third time they'd made love had been only a couple of hours before daybreak. It had been a magical night, the most magical she'd ever spent. He had certainly lived up to every fantasy that had ever crossed her mind.

She returned to the kitchen and poured herself a cup of coffee. She chuckled to herself at the realization that she was now making coffee stronger to suit Jace's taste rather than hers, even though he was not there to drink it. That wasn't the only change in her behavior that had occurred since arriving at the ranch, nor the only compromise in her outlook.

She had always been so in control of everything, but for the past couple of months it seemed that her life had started to unravel in spite of that and she didn't know how to stop it. Part of her last-minute trip to see Jerry Kensington had been an effort to put things back together.

She had done a lot of reading in an attempt to gather a better understanding of what had been happening to her. One book stated that compulsives were able to manage all the dynamics in their lives as long as everything was in place, much like a juggler keeping all the balls moving in a pattern. As long as the compulsive personality was able to handle all the facets at once, then they were able to function seemingly without any problems. But if something got out of whack, such as one too many objects for the juggler to work into the pattern, then it could easily fall apart, leaving the juggler floundering while trying to establish that smooth flow again.

The discovery of her fiancé's betrayal had upset the pattern's flow. Before she could get her balance back, Jace Tremayne had become an additional object. His intrusion into her neatly ordered existence had been responsible for finally toppling her carefully controlled juggling act, and she didn't know what to do about it.

She rinsed out her coffee cup and set it in the sink. She was about to do yet one more thing totally out of character. She took some apples and raw carrots, cut them into large pieces, put them in a plastic bag and placed it on the kitchen counter for later. Next she changed into the warm winter clothes Jace had provided her, pulled on the snow boots and warm jacket and opened the front door to the cold. She hurried across the yard to the barn. Much to her relief, neither Jace nor anyone else seemed to be inside.

First were the chickens. She was more determined than ever to conquer this major obstacle. She would feed them, then collect *all* the eggs without breaking any. She filled the feed bucket and marched into the henhouse without hesitation.

"Here chick, chick, chick. It's time for breakfast." She deposited the feed without incident, then replaced the feed bucket and picked up the egg basket. She paused at the door, squared her shoulders, took a deep breath and shoved ahead.

She marched directly to the first nest, her sights totally focused on her destination and the task at hand. A little tremor of anxiety darted through her body as she reached for the egg. Then there was a second egg and a third. Before she realized it, she was finished. She returned to the kitchen with her prize, washed the eggs and placed them in the bowl. The feeling of accomplishment associated with the simple chore far outweighed the many achievements from her career. Maybe gathering eggs was not a very challenging task in the world at large, but it had been a major triumph for her, and she felt good about it.

She grabbed the plastic bag of apple and carrot pieces and made her way to the stables. A couple of the ranch hands nodded acknowledgment of her presence as they hurried toward their own daily chores. She had never been to the stables before, but she could tell from the outside of the large building that it was a lot more than just horse stalls. She cautiously opened the door, not at all sure what—or who—she would find inside.

She stepped into the large, cavernous structure. In the middle of the room was an exercise ring, and along the outer walls were about forty horse stalls. The ranch was obviously a first-class and very successful operation that could afford an indoor horse ring and a helicopter. For the first time she wondered just how large the ranch was. For the first time she wondered several things, and chief among them was what it would be like to live on a ranch full-time, if she would be able to make the adjustment.

She heard voices coming from the far end of the building. Three of the ranch hands were grooming horses. She slowly made her way in their direction, taking time to pause at each occupied stall. Each horse received a friendly stroke on the neck, a whispered endearment and either an apple piece or chunk of carrot. She ran out of treats just as she reached the grooming area.

"Morning, ma'am." One of the cowboys tipped his hat when she approached. A slight wrinkle of confusion furrowed his brow. "Something I can do for you?"

"No...nothing, thank you."

"If you don't mind my saying so, ma'am, I'm a might surprised to see you out in this kind of weather."

"I guess I was experiencing a little touch of cabin fever." Her gaze darted around the grooming area. The other two men were watching and listening, as if they were anticipating that she would say something revealing. "I'm not accustomed to being cooped up for days at a time. I needed to get out."

"Yes, ma'am." The three men returned to their work, leaving her to her own devices.

"Uh, excuse me. I hate to bother you again."

One of the men looked up. "Yeah?"

"Do you know where I can find Vince?"

"He's probably in the garage. Out this door—" he gestured with the curry comb he had been using, "—next building over."

"Thank you." Samantha went in the direction indicated. She entered the garage and immediately spotted the Sno-Cat she had seen the day before. Among the other vehicles were snowmobiles, four-wheel-drive pickup trucks, a large tractor with a front-end snowplow attachment, and another truck with a large flatbed and removable stake sides. All of these carried the ranch's logo and name.

In addition to the work vehicles there was a brand-new Ford Explorer that she assumed to be Jace's personal car. Parked next to it, appearing totally out of place among the newer vehicles and work fleet, was a red Ford pickup truck that had obviously been lovingly polished and maintained over the years. Jace had mentioned one morning over breakfast that he still had the first vehicle he'd ever owned, and this old truck was apparently that sentimental possession.

On the far side was a large machine that she took to be the generator Jace had mentioned. Other implements and assorted pieces of machinery were scattered about. She spotted an older man in the corner diligently working on something.

She called out to him. "Vince?"

He turned around and scowled in her direction. "Yep."

"Jace said it was you who braved this storm to get my suitcase. I want to thank you for your efforts. I was sure surprised when I saw it, and I can't tell you how much I appreciate having my—"

"Weren't no trouble." With that Vince turned back to his work, indicating that the conversation was over.

Samantha was taken aback by his abrupt attitude, but figured that it was just his way. "Well...uh, thank you." When Vince didn't acknowledge her comment, she turned and left the garage. It had been a very productive day so far. However, she had one more conquest before she could return to the house, and that challenge was Emmylou.

She went to the barn, but was dismayed to see Emmylou's stall empty. Then she noticed the cow a couple of stalls down. She assumed that someone had moved Emmylou in order to clean out the stall. She found the milk stool and pail and positioned herself to go to work.

The cow seemed fidgety, constantly stepping back and forth as Samantha tried to reach under her. She finally grabbed hold. The cow immediately brushed against her, knocking her off the stool. She jumped to her feet, brushing the dirt and straw from her clothes. "Emmylou...what's the matter with you? Have you forgotten me? Why won't you let me milk you?"

"Well...in the first place that's not Emmylou."

Samantha whirled around at the sound of Jace's voice. Even though his face held a stern expression, amusement twinkled in his eyes. "I...I didn't hear you. Have you been there long?" She felt the flush of embarrassment spread across her cheeks again, something that had been happening far too often of late.

"Long enough." He walked around the partition and joined her in the stall. "This—" he patted the cow's rump "—is Betsylou. She's already been milked, so your efforts wouldn't have produced any results...other than a very unhappy cow."

The feeling became more intimate as he drew her into his embrace. "What are you doing out here?"

She glanced down at the ground for a second. She wasn't sure how to explain her activities. "I wanted to try to do the barnyard chores again. To see if I could get them right this time. You know, feed the chickens and collect the eggs without making a total mess of the henhouse."

"I understand you were sneaking little treats to my horses, too."

She stared at him for a minute, her brow wrinkling into a frown as she pursed her lips. "Does everyone report back to you every time I step foot out of the house?"

He took a step back, half serious and half in fun, as he threw his arms up in protest. His voice teased, but his words carried a more serious tone to them. "Rein in that temper of yours before we end up in some sort of argument again. I was just at the stables. I wanted to check on that roof patch. The boys mentioned that you had been there. Apparently they were surprised that a city girl had ventured out in the storm."

"A city girl? I'll have you know that I'm not a helpless—"

"I know, you're not a helpless little ninny. You mentioned that before and I believe you."

"But you do think I'm more of a nuisance than a help, tactfully suggesting that I might be more comfortable if I stayed in the house. Well, I'll have you know that so far this morning I've fed the chickens and collected *all* the eggs without incident. I think that should prove to you that I'm—"

Surprise clouded his features. He was obviously taken aback by her words. "You don't need to prove anything, Samantha. Certainly not to me, or to anyone else for that matter." He reached out and brushed his fingertips against her cheek. "Don't try to be what you think someone else wants you to be. All you have to do is be who you are." He placed a loving kiss on her lips as if to stop anything she might have started to say.

Emotion welled inside her. She fought to keep the tears from her eyes. It was the first time in her life anyone had ever told her that it was all right for her to just be herself, that it was acceptable and even preferable. Jace was a very special man, who had a very profound effect on her life.

His voice took on a soft, sensual quality. "I thought you were going to stay in bed and catch up on your sleep." A wry grin tugged at the corners of his mouth. "I know you couldn't have gotten any more sleep than I did."

She put her arms around his waist and leaned her head against his chest. "I admit I could have used another couple of hours of sleep."

"I'm sorry if I kept you awake. You should have told me you were too tired. I would have understood. I wouldn't have been particularly happy about it, but I would have understood."

She looked up at his face. Even though the conversation was an intimate one, she saw the teasing glint in his eyes. She couldn't stop the smile that spread across her face as she answered him. "I may be a little tired right now, but I wouldn't have missed last night for all the sleep in the world."

The teasing glint disappeared, and a worried look came into his eyes. His expression was cautious, his voice tentative. "Are you sure? I've been concerned...worried that I might have somehow failed to provide you what you wanted...needed." He cradled her head against his shoulder. "Oh, Samantha..." He whispered her name in the form of a sigh, as if he hadn't realized he had said it aloud.

She sought to reassure him, his sudden admission of vulnerability touching her deeply. "Last night was perfect. The word *failed* shouldn't even be part of the same conversation."

He had expressed a concern about satisfying her needs. It was something she wasn't used to, someone putting her needs first. It was one of the things she loved about him. He didn't put on airs or hide behind pretenses. Her thoughts came to a crashing halt. Had she actually used the word *love?* Where could it have possibly come from?

She had known this man such a short time. They both knew she was at the ranch on a purely temporary basis. They had discussed the fact that she would be leaving as soon as the roads were cleared. A sudden and overwhelming sadness engulfed her. She did not want to leave.

Even with the restrictions imposed by the storm and the fact that she found herself in totally unfamiliar surroundings and circumstances, she had to admit that these last few days had been the most stress free she had spent in many years. The disagreements with Jace, coupled with the inconvenience of being trapped in a strange place without any of her personal belongings, had not dampened the sense of freedom and inner peace that being at his ranch had produced.

Jace took her hand in his. "Come on, let's go back to the house."

"I don't want to interfere with your work. I can get back by myself."

"The boys have things well in hand, and all the emergencies are under control. So, I'd much rather spend what's left of the day having you tell me all about yourself."

The idea caused her to laugh out loud. "There's really not very much to tell that you don't already know, certainly nothing very interesting."

He squeezed her hand. "You don't know what it is

that I find interesting. Why don't you let me judge for myself?''

They stepped out of the barn and into the snowy afternoon…hand in hand. Jace came to an abrupt halt and looked up into the sky, then over to the weather vane on top of the barn.

Samantha tried to figure out what he was looking at, but couldn't make sense of it. "What's the matter? Is something wrong?''

He looked at her, then back into the sky. "Can't you feel it?''

"What?''

"The storm…I think we're on the waning side. The wind has calmed considerably, and the snowfall has decreased by at least half. We might be out of this by tomorrow.''

She saw how pleased he was and she tried to match his enthusiasm. "That's great. The repair crews will be able to get out and restore the power.'' *And the highway department can plow out the roads and then I'll be able to get my car and—* No, she didn't want to project any further into the future. It was a future that seemed to hold only sadness.

"Come on. Let's see if we can get the latest weather report on the battery radio.'' He hurried toward the house with Samantha practically running to keep up with his long-legged stride.

The burning logs popped and crackled in the fireplace in Jace's bedroom. He pulled Samantha's body closer to his as they snuggled beneath the covers. It had been an enlightening afternoon and evening as they'd each learned more about the other, but there was no mistaking the erotic overtones that permeated the air.

He ran his hand down her back. "You have the smoothest skin." Then he trailed his fingers across the roundness of her bottom. "And it covers the most delightful curves." He dipped his head until he was able to tease her nipple with his tongue. He slowly drew it into his mouth, held it there for a moment, then released the bud. "Mmm...and it tastes as good as it feels."

Samantha closed her eyes and allowed the warmth of his touch to spread over her. The previous night's intimacies were still very vivid in her mind, and his touch brought them back full force. She felt so open, completely free of any inhibitions. Everything about her life had been controlled. Even her lovemaking with Jerry Kensington had been more mechanical than spontaneous—not at all the fever of excitement she had shared with Jace.

A new sense of daring tickled her reality and produced an almost scandalous thought. If last night's cautious foray was risqué, then what she was about to do defied description. She placed a soft kiss on his chest, trailed her tongue down to his navel, then closed her lips around his rapidly hardening manhood. She felt his entire body stiffen, then his hips bucked upward.

At first Jace was not sure exactly what she had in mind, but whatever it was he planned to thoroughly enjoy it. Then the moist warmth of her mouth enveloped his passionate need. An incredibly sensual jolt of rapture shot through his body, causing him to literally lift off the bed. A growl of almost unbearably intense hedonistic gratification clawed its way out of his throat.

He thought the previous night had attained a level of sensual satisfaction beyond anything he had hoped for. But this...his surprise was only exceeded by his keen appreciation of Samantha's ability to excite him as no

one else ever had before. He relished every second of
her seductive attentions as she propelled him closer and
closer to the edge.

Making love was a time of closeness, a time of sharing. He knew if he planned to have anything left to
share, he needed to pull back from her now, no matter
how much he wanted more of the tantalizing sensations
she stirred deep inside him. His muscles, his strength,
the very essence of what held him together quivered with
an almost uncontrollable spasm of delight. He reached
down and gently but firmly pulled her body up onto his.

His words were so thick with the depth of the passions
boiling inside him that he hardly recognized his own
voice. "If you don't stop that exquisite torture this minute, the evening will end much too soon." He kissed her
throat and nuzzled the side of her neck. "And I want
this evening to last for a very long time."

Samantha trembled with desire, his words exciting her
as much as his touch. She wanted the evening to last for
a long time, too. She wanted it to last forever. Before
another thought could form, his mouth captured hers
with a kiss hot enough to set the bed on fire.

She ran her fingers through his hair as he crushed her
body to his. Slick, moist skin pressed against slick, moist
skin. The sounds of heavy breathing mingled with the
moans of two people totally immersed in the throes of
wanton desires.

The pulse of her life force called out to his soul the
moment he entered her. Their hips moved in sync propelled by the rhythm of his thrusting, each stroke bring-
ing them together in an ethereal oneness. Time stood
still, yet at the same instant it rushed by at a lightning
speed. Only their togetherness mattered, the sharing of

the physical bond coupled with the emotional ties that drew them closer and closer with each passing second.

Samantha teetered on the brink between the existence of here and now and the euphoric intoxication that was only a moment away. All reality ceased to exist except for the very real intensity of Jace's body covering hers and his manhood embedded inside her.

The force of her convulsions pulled him farther in, emotionally as well as physically. The tenuous hold he had on his control disappeared in an incendiary flash. The hard spasms shuddered through his body, finally subsiding and leaving him spent and exhausted...yet at the same time more alive than he had ever been.

They remained in each other's arms for the rest of the night. They slept for short periods at a stretch and shared quiet conversation while intimately touching and caressing each other during those awake times. Morning came too soon. It meant they had to leave the comfort and warmth of Jace's bed and put their shared intimacies aside for the day.

It meant something else, too. As soon as Samantha saw the sun shining brightly in the blue sky, she knew the time was very near when she would have to leave. Jace had been right. The wind had stopped blowing, the snow had stopped falling, and the clouds had disappeared. Now it was just a matter of time until the roads were cleared and she would be free to go. But, go where? To Los Angeles and her corporate clients? To freeway rush hour traffic and parking lots with no empty spaces? To her regimented and carefully controlled lifestyle?

She belonged back at work where she knew what she was doing and what to expect from the people around her. She belonged in an atmosphere where she functioned comfortably and efficiently. But could she ever be truly happy there again? An overwhelming sadness settled over her. She knew the answer whether she was willing to admit it or not.

Jace headed toward the front door, intent on getting to the bunkhouse before the ranch hands started their day. Now that the storm had passed, they needed to dig out from under the accumulation of snow and do a thorough check for any damage. It looked to be a very busy couple of days. He was thankful for the added work load, something extra to take his mind off what he knew was the inevitable.

The clearing of the storm would allow the ranch to return to its normal operations. That part was good. But it also meant that the roads would once again be passable. Samantha would be free to leave, to return to her home, and he didn't know what to do to prevent it. He didn't know what to say to her; he wasn't even sure what he wanted to say. All he knew for sure was that he did not want her to leave—not now, not ever.

He paused at the front door, his hand on the doorknob. He had work to do, but he couldn't force himself to leave just yet. He leaned forward, his head resting against the doorjamb. "Samantha..." The depth of his emotion showed in his voice. "We have to talk—" He turned toward her, his words cut off in midsentence. A hauntingly sad expression covered her face, one that tugged at his heart at the same time that it alarmed him.

He rushed to her side, his concern for her shoving aside his own thoughts. "What's wrong?"

"Huh?" He startled her. She was so absorbed in her own thoughts that she didn't realize he'd been looking at her. She tried valiantly to cover up the awkward situation she had created. "Nothing...nothing's wrong."

She attempted to produce a confident smile, but knew she fell miserably short of her goal.

He drew her into his embrace, placing a tender kiss on her forehead. "Tell me what's bothering you, and don't say *nothing*. I can see it in your face as clearly as if you had said something."

"I...I guess I was just thinking about what was going to happen now." She tried to recover from her near slip of saying what she really felt. "You know, all the stuff that has to be done now that the storm is over. I was..." She brightened as a sudden ploy to divert his attention came to mind. "I was wondering what I could do to help."

He studied her, noted the nervousness in her eyes and the way she was unable to hold his gaze. "I'm not buying that, Samantha."

Jace brushed a soft kiss across her lips. A nervous twinge pricked at his stomach. "The storm has passed by. The roads will soon be open. You know as well as I do that by tomorrow everything will be different." He closed his eyes for a moment and took a calming breath. "We have to talk. Let's sit down after dinner. That way we won't be interrupted."

He saw the objection start to form in her eyes, then her acquiescence, before she glanced down at the floor. Her words came out as a soft whisper accompanied by a sigh of resignation. "Yes, we need to talk."

Ten

Jace squeezed Samantha's hand reassuringly and extended a confident smile. "Will you be okay?"

She returned the squeeze and the smile. "Yes. I'm going to feed the chickens, collect all the eggs and milk both cows. That should free up someone's time to help with the clean-up work."

The trepidation showed in his voice. "That's not necessary."

"I know it's not necessary, but I think I finally have it figured out. You'll see...there won't be any problems." She mustered all the confidence she could find as she turned him toward the door. "Now get to work."

He laughed, amused at her take-charge attitude. "Yes, ma'am." It had such a comfortable feel about it...him leaving yet knowing she would be there when he returned, that they would be together for the entire night.

Jace embarked on his day and Samantha prepared for

hers. They each made a concerted effort to not dwell on things beyond the immediate. But no matter how much they tried, the specter of what had to be lurked around every corner and behind every tree.

The air reverberated with the noise from the snow-blowers and the shouts of men trying to put things back to normal. Little by little open areas of the yard and the walkways between buildings were cleared. Ben checked the fencing around the corral.

Jace fired up the helicopter and lifted off for an aerial inspection of the ranch. He flew the fence line to look for any obvious problems that needed immediate attention. He checked the herds in the outlying pastures, noting that his neighbor had taken care of the necessary feed drop as agreed upon. Next he turned toward the road.

He flew low over the snow-covered roadway until he came to Samantha's car. He hovered above the automobile, peering through the swirl of snow kicked up by the copter's rotor blade. Nothing seemed amiss. He assumed the car battery would be dead, but hopefully nothing else had been damaged.

He would have Vince check it over and fix whatever was wrong. Even though it was a rental car, there was no local office for the rental agency. He knew Samantha would have some financial liability for any problems, even if it was nothing more than a deductible payment for the insurance company. If he made the car road-worthy again, then it would save her that money and aggravation. He ignored the nagging voice that told him his own aggravation at her leaving could not be as easily handled.

The afternoon started to fade into evening. Jace turned the copter toward home. No sooner had he set down than

Ben grabbed his attention. The two men headed for the barn.

"I don't want you to think I was spyin' on your houseguest, but I happened to be working around the feed bins when she came in." Ben preceded Jace through the barn door.

It seemed to Jace that Ben was taking an inordinately long time to get to his point. He was not sure whether to be irritated or alarmed. "Do you have some point here somewhere? Is there a problem of some sort?"

"Well, no...no problem." Ben appeared genuinely confused by Jace's sharp attitude. "I just wanted to tell you that after a bit of a rocky start she managed to milk both cows and she did a pretty fair job of it." Ben stared at Jace for a moment before speaking again. "Are you all right? Did you find a lot of damage while you were out?"

"No, no apparent damage." Jace knew he had sounded too sharp. It wasn't Ben's fault. His helicopter tour told him it would not be very long before Samantha would be free to leave, maybe only one more day. As much as he tried to keep his mind on ranch business, he had spent most of his time agonizing over what seemed to him to be a no-win situation.

In an abrupt and uncharacteristic change of pace he whirled around and headed back for the door, calling over his shoulder as he went. "Where's Vince?"

Ben called after him, making no effort to catch up with wherever Jace was going. "He's in the bunkhouse washing up."

"I'll see you later." Jace disappeared through the door and out into the evening air, leaving Ben staring after him with a perplexed expression on his face.

* * *

Samantha had tried her best to keep busy all day so she would not have time to think about the future. She concentrated on collecting eggs and making friends with the chickens. She gave her best effort to milking the cows. She gathered clothes to do her laundry, but was stopped by the fact that the power had not yet been restored.

Now it was evening, the last of the daylight fading away. She lit one of the oil lamps and placed it in the living room, then sat down and waited. Jace was right, they needed to talk. As much as she tried to formulate her thoughts and gather the proper words, nothing jelled for her. In spite of all the pitfalls and awkward situations that had surrounded her stay at the ranch—the most troublesome being her sense of having no control over anything—and even the fact that the weather had kept her pretty much confined to the house, she knew she was going to miss it very much.

However, she didn't see any way that she could pick up, move to Wyoming and start all over. It simply wasn't practical or logical. She knew she would never be able to reestablish her career in a place where it appeared she would be lucky to find any work at all in her field, let alone enough to financially support herself. She still didn't know how close she was to a large town where she could even hope to find a satisfactory job.

She fully realized the direction her thoughts were headed. She was treating the situation as if she were already on her way back to Los Angeles. She didn't know what else to do. To rationally think about the implications of leaving and explore the alternatives would cost her too much emotionally. It needed to be a clean break. Besides, Jace hadn't said anything to her that indicated he even wanted her to stay.

Perhaps they were nothing more than two ships passing in the night, two people who were physically attracted to each other and had played out their sensual fantasies to their mutual enjoyment. She knew for her that it was much more, but she needed to face reality. She had always been able to collect facts, analyze the data, study a situation from all angles and make an intelligent and logical evaluation. For the past few days, however, she had lived in an entirely different world— a world of doing rather than thinking about it. It had started out rocky, but she had grown comfortable with it in a surprisingly short time.

She leaned her head back and closed her eyes. She needed to put all of that behind her. There was nothing practical or logical about her even toying with the idea of staying. She would return to Los Angeles as soon as the roads were cleared. The parting of the ways would happen soon enough without her dwelling on it.

And when it happened she knew it would break her heart.

She was tired, emotionally tired. Somewhere in the back of her mind she wondered where Jace was, why he hadn't come back to the house. After that, things drifted into darkness as an uneasy sleep claimed her.

While Samantha dozed in the living room easy chair Jace and Vince were hard at work. They had taken out the Sno-Cat, towing the large flatbed sled used to haul feed to cattle in the outlying pastures during winter. They made good time across the open landscape even with the handicap of darkness, finally arriving at the location where Samantha's car was stuck in the snow. They dug out around the car, then winched it up on the large sled and took it back to the garage.

* * *

Jace paced back and forth, pausing every few steps to peer over Vince's shoulder. He finally stopped behind Vince and watched for a couple of minutes. "Well, what's the verdict?"

Vince turned around and stared at Jace, his look and tone of voice showing his irritation. "Don't know yet. Won't know until you leave me alone long enough to check it out."

"Yeah...sorry." He wasn't sure if he wanted the car to be in good shape or if he wanted it to require a few days for repairs so she would be forced to stay. Jace plopped down on a bench, his mood changing from impatient to almost sullen as he waited to find out what his immediate future held.

It seemed like forever before Vince gave him the news. "Looks like it's just the battery. Replace that, wash the car and it'll be good as new...for a rental car."

"Would you take care of that for me?"

Vince tendered a hesitant question. "You want it tonight?"

Jace chuckled at his mechanic's guarded tone. "Tomorrow will be fine, Vince. See you in the morning."

Jace returned to the house. It had been a very long day and he was tired. His exhaustion was as much emotional as physical. Every time a thought about Samantha actually leaving the ranch—leaving him—managed to penetrate his consciousness, it took an extra effort for him to shove it aside, each time becoming more difficult than the last.

As soon as he entered the living room he spotted Samantha curled up in his chair. Even though she appeared to be asleep, her face held an uneasy look—a troubled expression that sent a quiver of apprehension through his body and made him feel decidedly uncomfortable.

He studied her for a moment, torn between wanting to crush her body tightly against his and not wanting to disturb her.

He toyed with the idea of telling her it would be several days before her car was fit to drive, but dismissed the idea as stupid. He certainly could not prevent her from calling the rental car agency, and even though they did not have a local office he was sure they would send someone to pick up the car and tow it away if they thought major repairs were involved. It was definitely a lousy idea. Somehow, someway he had to think of a plan...something to make it necessary for her to stay a while longer.

He knew exactly where his thoughts were headed. It frightened him, but this time he didn't back off from it. He didn't understand how she could have become so important to his life in such a short time, but the undeniable truth was that she had. They needed to talk, to reach some kind of solution...as long as that solution resulted in her staying at the ranch. He tightly clenched his jaw in reaction to his uncharacteristically domineering thoughts. Did he have the right to expect her to give up her career and a lifestyle she obviously preferred and enjoyed in order to stay with him? What did he have to offer her?

He steeled himself with a new sense of determination. He had been given a second chance at happiness, and he wasn't going to let it go without a fight.

He didn't have time to give it any more thought. Samantha stirred in her sleep, apparently seeking a more comfortable position in the chair. Her brow wrinkled, and a grimace crossed her face. Jace went to her. Whatever was going through her mind, it certainly wasn't anything pleasant.

He gently scooped her up in his arms. She unconsciously snuggled against his body, her head resting on his shoulder. They needed to talk, but obviously it would have to wait until a later time. He placed a light kiss on her forehead as he carried her down the hallway toward his bedroom. The past two nights had been very important to him, far more than just making love with a beautiful, exciting woman. Waking up in the morning with Samantha beside him had given his life a vibrant new meaning that he thought had been lost to him forever. Now that he'd found that, now that he knew it was all right for him to love again, he didn't want to lose it.

Something awakened Samantha. She remained still, with her eyes closed as she tried to clear the fog from her head. She became aware of Jace's arm around her and found immediate comfort from the warmth of his body as he slept next to her.

She didn't know how she would be able to face her cold, sterile apartment and her impersonal job. In fact, her entire life had been impersonal. She'd been merely existing, moving from one goal to the next in an effort to garner the approval of others. She wanted so much more from Jace...she wanted his love.

She sat up. There it was again...the sound that had awakened her. She listened. It was the stereo and there was light coming from down the hallway. The electricity had been restored. She carefully pulled back the covers and scooted toward the edge of the bed. She wanted to slip out without waking Jace. She would hurry down the hall, turn off the light and stereo, and be back in bed in less than a minute. That was her intention. She swung her legs over the edge of the bed. A hand grabbed her arm and pulled her back.

Jace's voice was thick with sleep. "I hear music."

"There's light, too. The electricity's back on. I was going to turn off the lamp and stereo."

He pulled her into his arms and nuzzled his face in her hair. "It can wait until morning."

A soft, sensual warmth spread through her body as she returned his embrace. "Yes, it certainly can."

They held each other, nothing more. Each was comfortable in the physical and emotional closeness, without the need to hear reassurances from the other. It took only a few minutes for them to once again succumb to sleep.

When morning finally came they remained in bed cuddled together beneath the blankets. It was Samantha who finally broached the subject that weighed heavily on each of their minds.

"Now that power has been restored, I would imagine that—" The words caught in her throat. She didn't want to say them. More accurately, she didn't want to deal with the implications of what they meant. "Uh...I guess the roads will be cleared soon."

"Yes. Depending on where the power lines came down, the road where your car was stuck might already be cleared." He felt the shiver run through her body. He held her closer, placing a loving kiss on her cheek before twining his fingers in her hair.

"Jace...I, uh..."

"Yes?" Apprehension twisted in the pit of his stomach. The time had come. She was about to tell him she would be returning home. And he didn't know how to stop her.

"It's...is there someone to call to find out about the roads? About when I'll be able to get my car? I might have to call the rental agency if the car won't run." She didn't want to start a conversation about leaving. That would come soon enough. But her practical and logical self said she needed to tend to the business of the rental car. When she'd waived the additional insurance coverage from the rental company, she'd become financially liable.

He held her close, not wanting to release her just yet. He was strong. He was assertive. He was accustomed to making quick and decisive judgments—instant decisions followed by immediate action. Yet this one had him floundering around like a fish out of water.

"Actually..." He took a deep breath in an attempt to calm his nerves. "Your car is okay. It just needed a new battery." He felt her body stiffen.

"How do you know?" An uneasiness settled over her, a nervous tremor that told her the inevitable could not be put off any longer.

"Last night...Vince and I went out and brought it back, and he checked it over."

She managed to wiggle out of his embrace and sit up. "You've already retrieved my car? The roads were open?"

"I don't know which roads are open, if any. We took the Sno-Cat and feed sled out across the pasture."

"Oh, I see." All of her hopes crashed inside her. He was ready for her to leave. He'd even picked up her car for her. There was no longer anything for them to talk about. "Well, it seems there's nothing left to do except find out about the roads."

Jace watched in silence as Samantha left his bedroom and went down the hall to the guest room. Judging by what she'd said about checking on the road conditions, she was obviously ready to return to Los Angeles—to the world she knew and felt comfortable with. With a heavy heart he went to the bathroom and turned on the shower.

Samantha dressed, went to the kitchen and made coffee, then pulled on the snow boots and jacket. She wanted to feed the chickens and collect the eggs. It would most likely be her last chance. As much trouble as the simple task had given her, she felt a strangely fulfilling sense of accomplishment connected with it. She had conquered a fear and succeeded at something new and very foreign to her.

She stepped outside into the sunshine. Already the temperature felt warmer than it had the day before and it was still early morning. The walkways had all been cleared of snow, as had the corral where several of the horses seemed to enjoy being outdoors again. In just one day the place had been transformed from an isolated, snow-covered group of buildings, outwardly appearing to be without life, to a busy working ranch. She spotted half a dozen men doing different jobs, all of them already hard at work for the day.

She hurried toward the barn, pausing for a minute to talk to Denny. "As soon as I finish in the henhouse, I'll be milking the cows. Do you want me to bring the filled buckets to you?"

"Yes, ma'am. That'll be fine. I'll be over by the corral. You just give me a shout when you're through."

Samantha breezed through the feeding and egg collecting with relatively few problems. She took the eggs back to the kitchen, washed them and deposited them in the large bowl. She didn't see Jace anywhere. It was just as well. She planned to keep busy in hopes that the day would pass quickly and she would not have time to dwell on the emotional ordeal ahead of her.

She milked both cows, gave the buckets to Denny,

then wandered over to the corral to see the horses. The roar of an engine filled the air. She turned and spotted Jace coming toward her on a snowmobile. He pulled up next to her.

"Want to go for a ride? See a little bit of the ranch?" He was doing his best to project an upbeat manner. He wanted to show her the beauty of the countryside, the openness and tranquillity that he found so appealing…that he hoped she would find equally appealing.

She looked at the snowmobile. A hint of anxiety darted across her face. "I've never been on one of those before. I'm not sure I'd know how to drive it."

He indicated the padded leather seat behind him. "No problem. Hop on back here." He shot her a confident smile, but inside he was a mass of nerves. As he saw it, he had one shot at persuading her to stay, and he planned to make the most of it. He had been encouraged by the fact that she hadn't bothered to go to the garage to check on her car.

The idea had occurred to him while he was in the shower that morning. He'd packed everything he needed and taken it to his intended destination, then had come back for Samantha. He planned to take her to the lake and woo her with a romantic snow picnic.

She hesitated for a moment, then climbed on behind him. He revved the engine as she wrapped her arms around his waist, then he headed the snowmobile straight out across the open countryside. Half an hour later they came upon a small lake that reflected the brilliant blue of the sky.

Jace pulled up next to a large box that had been placed next to some rocks. He cut the engine on the snowmobile, dismounted and held his hand out to assist Samantha. He continued to hold her hand as they walked through the snow to the edge of the lake.

Mountains, forest, a sapphire blue lake, wide-open range…it seemed as if the entire world were spread out in front of her. She looked up to the sky, using her hand to shade her eyes from the sun. She heard the cry of a hawk, saw it circling high above. She closed her eyes and breathed deeply, taking the crisp, clean air into her lungs. She turned to Jace. "This is beautiful. Are we still on your ranch?"

"Yes." Jace put his arm around her shoulder. "I think this is my favorite spot. When I was a kid I'd come here to work out my problems. Then when I was older, I'd come here to think out critical decisions. Sometimes I'd come here when I just wanted to be alone with my thoughts or was troubled by something."

He pulled her into his arms and placed a soft kiss on her lips. "How about some lunch? Are you hungry?"

Her eyes widened in surprise. "Lunch? Here?"

"Sure." He flashed an inviting smile. "Where's your sense of adventure?" He indicated the large box. "I believe we have everything we need for a picnic."

Jace opened the box and produced a small, folding picnic table, a tablecloth, a bottle of wine and a picnic basket. It took him only a few minutes to get everything set up. He filled her glass with white wine, poured some into his own glass, then stuck the bottle into the snow to keep it chilled. He turned toward Samantha and offered his arm. "May I escort you to the table?"

She linked her arm with his. "Thank you, sir."

He tried his best to keep the conversation light and upbeat while being as charming as he knew how. At first she seemed a little reticent. If he'd learned nothing else about her, he knew that she was not quick to accept new ideas, and certainly not anything that was untried, untested and unproved. It took her a while to warm to an idea, to accept something that had not been carefully planned. He also knew that he did not have much time before even the secondary roads would be open.

They enjoyed a leisurely lunch, then lingered over their wine. Before he was ready for it, noon had become mid-afternoon. He couldn't delay the journey back much longer. He reluctantly began to gather the remnants of their picnic lunch.

She jumped to her feet and rushed to help him. "Here, let me do that. You prepared a marvelous picnic lunch. The least I can do is clean up."

He grabbed her hand to stop her, then pulled her into his arms. He searched her face for a moment, then settled on her eyes. He brushed her hair back from her face. He couldn't put it off any longer, yet he didn't have the slightest idea of how to say what he wanted. He took a calming breath.

"Samantha..." He leaned forward and placed a loving kiss on her lips. He didn't have a clue about how to tell her of his feelings, of how to ask her not to leave. He wasn't even sure exactly what it was he wanted to ask her. Did he want her to postpone her departure for a while, or did he want her to stay forever?

"I was wondering if...maybe you'd want to..." No doubt about it—he sounded like a blithering idiot. He couldn't manage any coherent sentences.

"Wondering what?" Her tightly knotted insides seemed to be stretched to their limit. Her breathing had turned ragged and difficult. She was so confused. Her logical and practical nature told her it was time to return

home and get on with her life. Her stay at his ranch had
been a delightful interlude, but the real world expected
her to return to her job and her responsibilities.

"I just thought that…well, perhaps you could—" He
captured her mouth with a demanding kiss.

Eleven

What started as an impulsive demanding kiss quickly turned soft and loving as Jace held Samantha in the warmth of his embrace. He twined his fingers in her hair and reveled in the feel of her body pressed against his. It had been a long time since he'd had a need to express his inner feelings. He fully knew how to demonstrate what he felt, but he didn't know how to say it. He also knew that he had better get it figured out before it was too late.

He finally released her from his kiss. He took her hand in his and walked to the edge of the lake. He sat on a large rock and pulled her down into his lap, then he looked out over the landscape as he gathered his words.

"There used to be a pair of swans who lived on this lake. They were beautiful to watch—their long graceful necks, the way they seemed to glide across the water. They were always together. When the geese would stop here for a few days during their spring and autumn migration flights, the male swan would ruffle his wings up and lower his head. He would patrol the water in an attack mode, making sure his mate was safe from all harm. Then one day something happened to the female swan and the male was left all alone. And since swans take one mate and one mate only, he remained alone for the rest of his life.''

"That's very sad. It's not fair that they can't have another mate." A touch of personal anguish tried to well inside her. "It's not fair that they can't be happy."

He took a deep breath and held it for a moment before releasing it. "Fortunately people aren't like swans. Even though they select a mate with the intentions of it being for life, if something happens they are free to choose another mate. They are allowed that second chance to find happiness again."

Full-blown panic gripped her in its clutches. She was not at all sure she wanted to hear any more. She heard what he'd said and she knew what he really meant. He was talking about her broken engagement, about her need to get on with her life. He was about to tell her that it was time for her to move on, for them to go their separate ways in search of a mate suited to their individual needs—for each of them to find happiness.

She felt the tremors of anxiety start in her stomach and quickly move outward. She knew she could not bear to hear him say the words of rejection. She had made a terrible mistake, allowing her own physical attraction to Jace to make her believe that he could feel something special for her. How was it possible for her to totally abandoned her logical and sensible way of doing things?

This was so unlike her, making assumptions without

gathering facts. But then, everything she'd done lately had been so unlike her, starting with her decision to go to Denver to see Jerry Kensington. It was obvious that this was not going to turn out any better than her ill-fated Denver excursion.

She had to put some distance between them before she embarrassed Jace and humiliated herself. She quickly rose from his lap and backed away a couple of paces. She glanced at her watch, then off toward the horizon. She tried to force a calm to her voice. "It's getting late. I think we'd better start back. I...I need to check on the road conditions." She began gathering their picnic leftovers and put everything back in the box.

Jace sat in stunned silence for a moment before he was able to move. Was this how things would end? He couldn't let it happen this way. There had to be something he could do, some way of changing her mind about leaving. But he didn't know what it was.

They rode back to the ranch house in silence, each lost in personal thoughts. Samantha started to go to the garage to see Vince, to check on her car, but changed her mind. Jace had told her it was fine. What she really needed was a map showing how to get back to the interstate highway. She went directly to the den while Jace put away the snowmobile.

She finally found a road map. She located where she was and marked the route to the highway and back to Denver. She would turn in the car and catch the next flight back to Los Angeles. There was no time for wasted efforts and misplaced sentimentality.

Suddenly every move she made seemed to be carefully planned out, just as her life had been before fate had deposited her in Jace Tremayne's backyard. Once again she functioned efficiently, taking care of all the necessary details. She checked the phone book for the number of the highway patrol, then called to get road information. The roads she had marked on the map were open. That meant she could leave right away. She knew she couldn't bear to spend another night in Jace's house—in his bed for one last time or alone in the guest room. It would be more heartache than she could handle.

Next she called the airline. She already had a paid ticket for her return flight, so all she needed to do was book a reservation. She would drive as far as she could, before stopping for the night, then continue on to the Denver airport the next morning where she needed to return her rental car. By tomorrow night she would be back home, back in her world, where she had control of her life. A shudder of sorrow over what might have been tried to work its way through her body, but she refused to allow it. She went to the guest room, closed the door and began packing her suitcase.

Jace stood in the hallway staring at her closed door. He had entered the house just in time to see her disappear into the bedroom. His tickle of uncertainty had turned into a burning need to tell her how he felt. He knocked at the closed door.

"Samantha? May I come in?" He waited, and when he didn't get a response he raised his hand to knock again. The door opened, and he saw Samantha with her suitcase in hand.

"I...uh...left the clothes you lent me—" she gestured behind her "—on the bed." She glanced away, unable to hold eye contact with him. "I guess I need to get on the road. I have a flight from Denver to Los Angeles late tomorrow afternoon."

He stood his ground, refusing to step aside so she could get through the door. "You're leaving? Right

now? Just like that? I thought we had things to discuss."
He took the suitcase from her, set it on the floor and
took her hand in his. He led her into the living room.
He felt her initial resistance, then she went with him.

He seated her on the couch, then sat next to her. Placing his fingertips beneath her chin, he lifted until he
could look into her eyes. He saw a myriad of emotions,
including wariness, apprehension, alarm…and an incred-
ible sadness.

"Are you really in such a hurry to get back to Los
Angeles, or is it that you just want to get away from
here…" His nervousness caused his voice to falter. "Or
are you in that much of a panic to get away from me?"

Her eyes widened in surprise. "Get away from you?
No…that's not it. It's just…well—" She turned away
from the penetrating gaze that again tried to pry into her
soul. "I have a job—"

"Weren't you listening when I was talking about the
swans? Didn't you understand what I was saying?" He
felt it slipping away. His words rambled around in cir-
cles without making any sense, and he didn't seem to
know how to stop. He couldn't get his words to come
out right, couldn't get them to match his feelings.

"Yes…I think I understood what you were saying."
Did she dare say what was going through her mind? Did
she dare express her hurt in words? "You were telling
me to put my broken engagement behind me and get on
with my life." A sob caught in her throat, but she forced
out the rest of the words. "You were telling me I'd been
here long enough and it was now time for me to go
home."

He grabbed her shoulders and stared at her. Relief,
anger, confusion…they all mingled together. "Is that
what you thought? That I was telling you to leave? How

could you have possibly thought that? Why in the world would I want you to leave?''

Shock covered her features. "But you said—''

"I was talking about me—about you and me and how lucky I was to have found a second chance, and when that happens it shouldn't be ignored.'' He took a calming breath. "Oh, God...I'm making a total mess out of this.'' He pulled her to him, wrapping her in a frantic embrace. "Samantha...I want you to stay.''

She didn't know what to say, how to respond. He had just taken what she thought and turned it inside out. The thought of staying was very attractive, but the reality was a different thing.

"I don't know what to say. Things aren't that easy for me.'' She closed her eyes and desperately tried to bring forth some sort of inner strength. "I need time to consider all the possibilities and to analyze the problem—''

"*Problem?*'' He released her and stumbled backward a couple of steps. The shock couldn't have been greater if she'd slapped him across the face. His words were tinged with the sting of his hurt. "I didn't realize this was nothing more to you than a *problem*, an intellectual exercise to be reduced to its basic elements so that you can study it and evaluate the many facets then come up with a logical response that is properly presented.''

"Jace...you don't understand—''

He was angry and he was hurt. He didn't know which at that moment was the stronger of the two emotions. "You're damn right, I *don't* understand. I thought we had something very special, something that could be used as a base to build a future. I guess I was wrong and you were right.''

"I was right about what?'' It was all she could do to

keep from crying. Her life seemed to be slipping through her fingers faster than quicksand and she couldn't stop it.

Pain surrounded his words, and sorrow filled his voice, signaling just how difficult the words were for him to say. "We're from two different worlds. We've always known that. Maybe it *is* time for you to return to your lifestyle and your world, to that place where people and feelings are apparently not very important." His final utterance trailed off to a barely discernible whisper, said more to himself than to her. "It was foolish of me to assume you could have been happy here...with me."

Jace took a few steps away, then turned back toward her. "Good luck to you, Samantha. I hope you find what you're searching for." He couldn't look at her without experiencing the most horrendous sense of loss. He left the house and hurried toward the stables. He was afraid to look back, afraid that he would end up making an even bigger fool of himself than he obviously already had. Whatever possessed him to think that someone like Samantha Burkett would want to give up a successful career to live on a cattle ranch?

He wandered around the stables, spending some time in the stall combing his horse and checking on the other horses. Then he heard the sound. The large door of the garage slid back, and he heard a vehicle drive away. He closed his eyes as the shudder moved through his body. He didn't know what to do. He tried to concentrate on ranch business, on the remaining work that needed to be done as part of the storm cleanup. Nothing helped. The only thing uppermost in his mind was Samantha.

He glanced at his watch. It had been almost an hour since she'd driven away. He had to make one last try.

She needed to follow the roads, but he could catch up
with her by flying cross-country. He charged out of the
stables, filled with a renewed determination.

He yelled out to his ranch foreman as he ran across
the yard. "Ben, I'm taking the copter up."

Ben whirled around, a surprised expression covering
his face. "Now? It'll be dark in an hour. What's up?"

Jace yelled back over his shoulder. "I'm not going to
be a swan if I can help it." With that he left a startled
Ben staring after him.

Ten minutes later Jace was in the air. When he finally
spotted her car, she was only a mile from the interstate.
There were no other noticeable cars in the immediate
area. He flew low over her car, then turned and hovered
above the road far enough ahead of her that she had
room to stop safely. He set the copter down in the middle
of the road in front of her stationary car.

Tears streamed down Samantha's cheeks and occasional sobs caught in her throat. She knew she had no
business driving in her emotionally fragile condition, but
she had to get as far away from Jace's ranch as possible,
before stopping for the night. She'd been arguing with
herself ever since passing through the front gate and
turning onto the road. Her logic and intellect told her
she was doing the right thing. Her heart tried to tell her
otherwise, but she refused to listen to it.

She heard the sound of the helicopter, then saw it in
front of her. She stopped her car, but didn't get out. As
much as she wanted to, she couldn't seem to force herself into action. A moment later she saw Jace ducking
under the rotor blade and running toward her. He
reached for her car door, yanked it open and pulled her
out of the car and into his arms.

His voice was soft, his words filled with the emotion that coursed through him. "Life doesn't give any guarantees, Samantha. If we want something, we need to act before it's too late, because we might not get another chance."

He placed a loving kiss on her lips. "I could not let you drive out of my life without telling you that I love you and I want very much for you to stay."

"Oh, Jace. I don't know what to do." She slipped her arms around his waist and rested her head against his shoulder. She felt the reassuring brush of his lips against her forehead. "Everything has happened so fast. I don't know how to cope with this. I need time to sort out my feelings. I have obligations, responsibilities—to my job, to my clients. I can't just *stay*." A sob caught in her throat. She couldn't say anything else.

"What about responsibilities to yourself? Emotions such as love cannot be analyzed with a computer, charted with a slide rule or taken under advisement while a two-year study is made. Don't you think you owe yourself the opportunity for happiness?"

She squeezed her eyes tightly shut in an effort to control her tears. Her words came out haltingly. "I have to go. I have to deal with this in the only way I know how." She looked up at his face. She saw the dejection and hurt in his eyes and the sorrow that blanketed his features. It cut right through to her heart. "We've only known each other for a week. I can't make a decision that will affect my entire life after knowing someone such a short time. There are so many unknowns, so many things..." She reached out a trembling hand and lightly touched his cheek. "I'm so sorry, Jace. I don't know what else to do."

He watched as she climbed back into her car and

drove around his helicopter. He continued to watch until she disappeared around the bend in the road.

She drove, her eyes on the road ahead but her mind elsewhere. She felt so helpless. She was caught between her responsibilities and her desires, between her obligations and her feelings. She knew she had just walked away from any chance of happiness—just as she had botched up every personal relationship in her life. But this hurt the most because she truly loved him. There was nothing logical or sensible about it. She could not come up with any concrete reason why it should be or why it would even work, but it was so.

The pounding noise finally penetrated Jace's sleep-clogged brain. It seemed that he had just gotten to sleep. He dragged himself out of bed and down the hallway. He opened the door. Standing on the porch, with suitcase in hand, was a very frightened-looking Samantha. He wasn't sure whether she was real or only part of the troubled dream that had been interrupted.

"May I come in?" Her voice was as frightened as she appeared.

"Of course." The fog cleared from his head, and reality took hold. He took her suitcase and pulled her inside the house, then kicked the door closed. His joy was tempered by his concern. "Are you all right?" He led her into the living room.

"Oh, Jace." She couldn't stop the tears. She melted into the warmth of his embrace. "I don't know what I am...other than incredibly stupid and stubborn. I got as far as the interstate and knew I had to come back. You were right. Life is more than facts and figures to be studied and analyzed, and love is something you feel rather than hold a meeting to discuss."

She looked up at him. "I don't care if I ever see another tailored, silk pantsuit or the inside of a conference room again. I promise I'll become friends with the chickens, and I'll even learn how to cook."

He couldn't stop the broad smile that slowly lit up his face. "If I didn't know you better, I'd say that sounded like an impetuous, rash promise—even bordering on spontaneous."

"I love you, Jace. I don't know how it happened, and I'm not even sure when, but I know it's true."

His expression turned serious. His voice held a slight quaver. "Are you sure, Samantha? Really sure?"

"I'm more sure than I've ever been of anything in my life. I'll stay as long as you want me to."

"I want more than for you to just stay...I want you to marry me. I want to know that you'll be here forever."

"Marriage?" Had she heard him correctly? "You want to marry me?"

"More than anything." He brushed his lips tenderly against hers.

"Yes." Her answer came without even a moment's pause.

He eyed her carefully. "You don't need time to think? I should warn you, cowboys are always tracking cowsh—" He stopped in midsentence, paused for a moment, then continued. "*Steer manure*, always tracking steer manure into the house."

"I'm flexible." She offered him a wry smile. "I can adjust."

"You're sure you want to?" His words were hesitant, as if he still wasn't convinced he'd heard her correctly.

"I'm sure." Her statement was definitive and final.

He picked up her suitcase, and they walked down the

hall together hand in hand. "I love you dearly, Samantha, but I think it might be better if you stayed away from the kitchen."

*   *   *   *   *

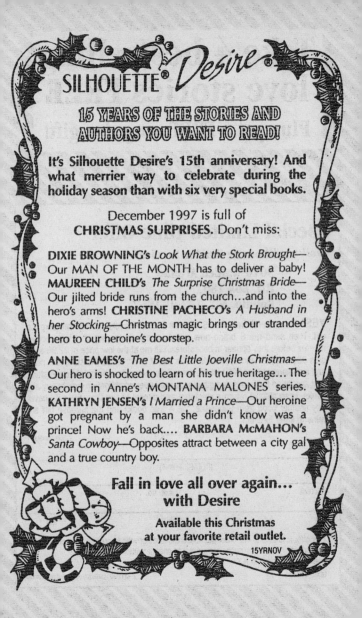

Take 4 bestselling love stories FREE
Plus get a FREE surprise gift!

Share in the joy of yuletide romance with brand-new
stories by two of the genre's most beloved writers

DIANA PALMER

and

JOAN JOHNSTON

in

LONE STAR CHRISTMAS

Diana Palmer and Joan Johnston share their favorite
Christmas anecdotes and personal stories in this
special hardbound edition.

Diana Palmer delivers an irresistible spin-off of her
LONG, TALL TEXANS series and Joan Johnston crafts an
unforgettable new chapter to **HAWK'S WAY** in this wonderful
keepsake edition celebrating the holiday season. So
perfect for gift giving, you'll want one for yourself...and
one to give to a special friend!

Available in November at your favorite retail outlet!

Only from

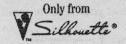

JJDPXMAS

Welcome to the Towers!

In January
New York Times bestselling author

NORA ROBERTS

takes us to the fabulous Maine coast mansion
haunted by a generations-old secret and introduces
us to the fascinating family that lives there.

Mechanic Catherine "C.C." Calhoun and hotel magnate
Trenton St. James mix like axle grease and mineral
water—until they kiss. Efficient Amanda Calhoun finds
easygoing Sloan O'Riley insufferable—and irresistible.
And they all must race to solve the mystery
surrounding a priceless hidden emerald necklace.

Catherine and Amanda
THE Calhoun Women

**A special 2-in-1 edition containing
COURTING CATHERINE and A MAN FOR AMANDA.**

Look for the next installment of
THE CALHOUN WOMEN with Lilah and Suzanna's
stories, coming in March 1998.

Available at your favorite retail outlet.

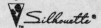 Silhouette®

SILHOUETTE WOMEN KNOW ROMANCE WHEN THEY SEE IT.

And they'll see it on **ROMANCE CLASSICS**, the new 24-hour TV channel devoted to romantic movies and original programs like the special **Romantically Speaking—Harlequin™ Goes Prime Time.**

Romantically Speaking—Harlequin™ Goes Prime Time introduces you to many of your favorite romance authors in a program developed exclusively for Harlequin® and Silhouette® readers.

Watch for **Romantically Speaking—Harlequin™ Goes Prime Time** beginning in the summer of 1997.

If you're not receiving ROMANCE CLASSICS, call your local cable operator or satellite provider and ask for it today!

ROMANCE CLASSICS

Escape to the network of your dreams.

See Ingrid Bergman and Gregory Peck in *Spellbound* on Romance Classics.

Help us celebrate
15 years of unforgettable romance with

▼ SILHOUETTE®

Desire®

You could win a genuine lead crystal vase, or one of 4 sets of 4 crystal champagne flutes! Every prize is made of hand-blown, hand-cut crystal, with each process handled by master craftsmen. We're making these fantastic gifts available to be won by you, just for helping us celebrate 15 years of the best romance reading around!

DESIRE CRYSTAL SWEEPSTAKES
OFFICIAL ENTRY FORM

To enter, complete an Official Entry Form or 3" x 5" card by hand printing the words "Desire Crystal Sweepstakes," your name and address thereon and mailing it to: in the U.S., Desire Crystal Sweepstakes, P.O. Box 9076, Buffalo, NY 14269-9076; in Canada, Desire Crystal Sweepstakes, P.O. Box 637, Fort Erie, Ontario L2A 5X3. Limit: one entry per envelope, one prize to an individual, family or organization. Entries must be sent via first-class mail and be received no later than 12/31/97. No responsibility is assumed for lost, late, misdirected or nondelivered mail.

DESIRE CRYSTAL SWEEPSTAKES
OFFICIAL ENTRY FORM

Name: _____

Address: _____

City: _____

State/Prov.: _____ Zip/Postal Code: _____

KFO

15YRENTRY

Desire Crystal Sweepstakes
Official Rules—No Purchase Necessary

To enter, complete an Official Entry Form or 3" x 5" card by hand printing the words "Desire Crystal Sweepstakes," your name and address thereon and mailing it to: in the U.S., Desire Crystal Sweepstakes, P.O. Box 9076, Buffalo, NY 14269-9076; in Canada, Desire Crystal Sweepstakes, P.O. Box 637, Fort Erie, Ontario L2A 5X3. Limit: one entry per envelope, one prize to an individual, family or organization. Entries must be sent via first-class mail and be received no later than 12/31/97. No responsibility is assumed for lost, late, misdirected or nondelivered mail.

Winners will be selected in random drawings (to be conducted no later than 1/31/98) from among all eligible entries received by D. L. Blair, Inc., an independent judging organization whose decisions are final. The prizes and their approximate values are: Grand Prize—a Mikasa Crystal Vase ($140 U.S.); 4 Second Prizes—a set of 4 Mikasa Crystal Champagne Flutes ($50 U.S. each set).

Sweepstakes offer is open only to residents of the U.S. (except Puerto Rico) and Canada who are 18 years of age or older, except employees and immediate family members of Harlequin Enterprises, Ltd., their affiliates, subsidiaries and all other agencies, entities and persons connected with the use, marketing or conduct of this sweepstakes. All applicable laws and regulations apply. Offer void wherever prohibited by law. Taxes and/or duties on prizes are the sole responsibility of the winners. Any litigation within the province of Quebec respecting the conduct and awarding of a prize in this sweepstakes may be submitted to the Régie des alcools, des courses et des jeux. All prizes will be awarded; winners will be notified by mail. No substitution for prizes is permitted. Odds of winning are dependent upon the number of eligible entries received.

Any prize or prize notification returned as undeliverable may result in the awarding of that prize to an alternative winner. By acceptance of their prize, winners consent to use of their names, photographs or likenesses for purposes of advertising, trade and promotion on behalf of Harlequin Enterprises, Ltd., without further compensation unless prohibited by law. In order to win a prize, residents of Canada will be required to correctly answer a time-limited, arithmetical skill-testing question administered by mail.

For a list of winners (available after January 31, 1998), send a separate stamped, self-addressed envelope to: Desire Crystal Sweepstakes 5309 Winners, P.O. Box 4200, Blair, NE 68009-4200, U.S.A.

Sweepstakes sponsored by Harlequin Enterprises Ltd., P.O. Box 9042, Buffalo, NY 14269-9042.

15YRRULE

Daniel MacGregor is at it again...

New York Times bestselling author

NORA ROBERTS

introduces us to a new generation of MacGregors
as the lovable patriarch of the illustrious MacGregor
clan plays matchmaker again, this time to his three
gorgeous granddaughters in

THE MACGREGOR BRIDES

From Silhouette Books

Don't miss this brand-new continuation of Nora Roberts's
enormously popular *MacGregor* miniseries.

Available November 1997 at your favorite retail outlet.

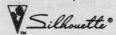